AFTER THE FINE WEATHER

Books by Michael Gilbert in Perennial Library:

AFTER THE FINE WEATHER

MICHAEL GILBERT

PERENNIAL LIBRARY

Harper & Row, Publishers
New York, Cambridge, Philadelphia, San Francisco
London, Mexico City, São Paulo, Singapore, Sydney

First PERENNIAL LIBRARY edition published 1988.

LIBRARY OF CONGRESS CATALOG CARD NUMBER: 88-45114

ISBN: 0-06-080935-3 (pbk.)

88 89 90 91 92 OPM 10 9 8 7 6 5 4 3 2 1

Contents

AFTER THE FINE WEATHER

1

Albin Boschetto

Lᴇɴɢʙᴇʀɢ ɪs ᴀ ᴄᴏᴍᴘᴀᴄᴛ ᴠɪʟʟᴀɢᴇ of red brick, red tile, and chestnut trees, dominated by the gaunt, yellowing prison built on its south-facing slope. It was from this prison that Albin Boschetto was released, at a quarter past eleven, on the morning of November 15.

Commandant Krimmer felt no regrets at Boschetto's departure. He had held him for three years, and in his view three years was enough. Boschetto was an Italian from the South Tyrol, large for his race, not corpulent, but tall and thick. He had black hair which, when free of prison discipline, would grow down into greasy ringlets almost to his collar; light-gray eyes; and a jaw which had been broken and set so badly that the bottom half of his face seemed to belong to a different man.

In the Commandant's view Boschetto was not entirely sane. He had said as much to Landesmin-

1

ister Drukl, who had visited the prison a month before and had shown interest in him and his record.

"A bad case of assault, Herr Landesminister. He held up a motorist, on the road to Villach, forced him at gunpoint to dismount, beat him on the head with the gun barrel, robbed him, kicked him, and left him for dead. I have a duplicate of the record if you would care to see it."

"I would rather see the prisoner," said the Landesminister.

They had walked together across the interior court, where privileged prisoners were tending the flower beds, and into the inner keep. Here it was dark and cold, and their feet fell softly on the fiber matting laid over the stone and iron-grated floor.

The Commandant slid back the shutter in the door. That part of the prison had been cut into the hillside. The cells received a ration of daylight and air, by a shaft, from above, but a light burned all day behind a thick glass set high in the ceiling.

Albin Boschetto sat on his bed. He was staring at the wall opposite him. He did not look happy. Nor did he look unhappy. He looked like an uncomplicated piece of machinery which has been laid, for the moment, to one side.

The Commandant felt Drukl shudder. "Yes, it is cold in here," he said. "You feel the difference, after the sunlight. Let us go back to the office."

"Does he always sit like that?"

"Oh, no. He has different moods. Sometimes he sings."

"Sings?"

"Marching songs. He was in a battalion with other Tyrolese during the war. At times he—well, he has habits that are less pleasant." He looked doubtfully at Drukl, and then decided that the dapper little man at his side, with the small, neat feet and the wispy beard, who had under his control all the prisons and prison officers in the Lienz district, must by now know something of the effects of prolonged imprisonment on simple men.

"To be specific . . ." he began.

Drukl listened to the recital impassively. Then he said, "They are a primitive race, the men from the High Tyrol. Unsuited to captivity. In my view there was something to be said for the old methods with such people. Liquidation might be kinder than incarceration."

Krimmer jerked his head up sharply. The Landesminister smiled at the look on his face. "I speak, of course, as a private person," he said, "not as a minister. He will be released—when?"

"On November fifteenth."

"Would you make a point of seeing, please, that all preliminaries are completed in good time, and that he is released at fifteen minutes past eleven."

"At eleven-fifteen."

"At *exactly* eleven-fifteen. It is not my request. I pass it on to you from its originator, Colonel Schatzmann."

Krimmer's face lost all outward expression. He said, in a carefully modulated voice, "Very well, Herr Landesminister. I will see that it is done."

3

And so at nine o'clock on November 15 Boschetto was led to the shower bath. His prison uniform was taken from him, and the clothes in which he had been arrested were returned to him, together with a pile of his possessions, which he checked and for which he scrawled some sort of receipt. The sum of four hundred and fifty Austrian schillings, which he had earned in prison, was handed to him. By eleven o'clock his documentation was completed, and the chief warder led him to the gatehouse. At eleven-fifteen the wicket gate opened and Boschetto stepped out onto the white dusty road.

He stood for a few moments, blinking and swinging his head from side to side. It was a lovely morning of high autumn. The fields were a patchwork of brown stubble and turned earth. The vineyards stood stripped and tidy. A frame of mist hung along the mountain, marking the limit of the early snow.

Albin Boschetto stumped off down the road toward Lengberg. In the distance a Volkswagen started up fussily and moved down a track toward the road. It was driven by a stout man in a dark-blue suit, who could not have been in a hurry, since he waited for quite five minutes before turning the nose of his car to the right and cruising down toward the roofs of Lengberg.

Boschetto was seated on a low wall at the crossroad outside the village, beside the halt sign for the Post Bus. He seemed indifferent to delay and content to relax in the sunshine. The only part of him

4

that moved was his tongue. Every few minutes it came out, licked round his lips, then took fright and disappeared. His big hands hung motionless by his side. Two boys, on their way home to lunch from school, came to the conclusion that he was worth a second look. They stopped to stare. Boschetto stooped, picked up a stone, and threw it with speed and precision. The boys scampered off down the road. Boschetto did not trouble to look after them. But the episode had broken his reverie. He fumbled in his pocket, got out a packet of cigarettes, and lit one.

The Volkswagen fussed through the village and passed Boschetto without stopping, the driver intent only on the road. Behind the car rolled the great yellow-and-silver Post Bus. Boschetto climbed aboard.

Half an hour later he dismounted in the main square at Lienz. By this time the Volkswagen was tucked into a line of cars on the other side of the square. Boschetto did not see it. Shouldering his pack, he strode out of the square toward the lower town. He walked straight ahead, paying no heed to other pedestrians. The pavement was crowded, and more than once a collision seemed imminent, but on each occasion it was the other man who stepped aside.

A hundred yards from the railway station he turned into a smaller road, walked quickly up it, crossed a footbridge over one of the branch lines, and turned into the road running parallel with it. It was one of the least agreeable quarters in the

5

town, a district of railway workshops, dirty cafés, drinking cellars, and brothels. Boschetto walked without a glance to right or left, though many eyes observed him, over raised glasses, through smeary windows, from behind lace curtains.

Near the end of the road, chipped white letters on a plate-glass window spelled out "Franzkeller." A step down led into the single front room. It smelled like the inside of a wine cask.

The thin man sitting behind the table jumped to his feet.

"Ernst!"

"Albin! I heard you were coming out today. Come in. Sit down. A drink?"

"Where's Clara?"

"In the kitchen. It was she who heard you were coming out." He was pouring wine into a glass as he spoke.

Boschetto put his pack carefully on the table, drank half the wine, and set the glass down beside the pack, then turned on his heel without a word, padded across the floor, and flung open the door.

There was a tiny scream from inside, though whether of joy or alarm it was hard to say. The door slammed shut. Ernst sat listening, his lips drawn back in a set smile. He heard the low rumble of Boschetto's bass and the higher notes of Clara, shrill with excitement and laughter. After a few minutes he heard the farther door, leading from the kitchen to the bedroom, open and then shut, cutting off the voices.

Ernst finished his own glass of wine. Then,

6

since it seemed intelligent to assume that his meal might be some time in coming, he emptied the half glass left by Boschetto. He was a careful man, who abhorred waste.

Next, he wandered across to the telephone that stood on a shelf behind the counter. It was coin operated, and the box was heavily padlocked. Ernst turned his attention to the till, sliding the drawer open half an inch and plunging his finger in to hold down the bell before opening it entirely. He extracted the schilling pieces that he wanted for the telephone and closed the drawer. Then he inserted the coins and dialed a number.

All his movements were gentle, and his brown eyes were soft as a spaniel's.

A female voice at the other end said something. Ernst asked for an extension number. A male voice growled.

"Ernst Radmacher. I am speaking from the Franzkeller Bar in Spargasse. Boschetto has arrived."

The voice said, "Yes."

Ernst said, "He is clearly very hungry. I should suppose that it will be some hours before his appetite is satisfied."

"Yes."

"Have you any further instructions for me?"

There was a pause, and then the voice said, "No," and there was a click as the receiver was replaced. Ernst sat for a moment rubbing his ear. It was almost as if he had been cuffed.

*   *   *

Colonel Julius Schatzmann, known, though not to his face, as the Gray Bear, stood behind his desk. Seventy-six inches separated his hair, which was cut short and en brosse, from his well-polished shoes. He was thick. His nose was thick, his lips were thick, and his neck was thick. A thick trunk was supported on thick thighs. He had button-bright eyes and a mischievous smile. The bear is one of the few animals known to have a sense of humor. Colonel Julius Schatzmann had a sense of humor. During his adventurous life he had found himself able to laugh at everything, even at his own discomfiture.

"Had I not been able to laugh," he said to his subordinate, Major Osler, "I should long ago have been dead. I laughed my way through the war, in the ranks of the SS, and I rose to be Feldwebel. I laughed at the occupying forces, with their tribunals and commissions, and they all left me alone. If you laugh at an American, he likes you. If you laugh at an Englishman, he respects you. If you laugh at a Frenchman, he hates you—but he too leaves you alone. Once—but only once—I remember, I laughed at Himmler."

"Not many people laughed at Himmler," said Major Osler.

"Not many. Now, to business, gentlemen. The Minister arrives by road from Vienna at seven o'clock this evening. I have, as you know, canceled all leave, withdrawn sleeping-out permits, and some weeks ago I made preliminary arrangements, which I trust are now well advanced, for calling out the auxiliary police."

"The arrangements are complete, sir. The men report to their depots tonight."

"Good. The parade is timed for eleven-thirty tomorrow. From nine o'clock all roads out of the town come under traffic control. Arranged, Inspector Biedermann?"

"Arranged, sir."

"To last until when?"

"My orders are that control shall continue until canceled by you."

"Very well. The approaches to the square are to be manned at ten-thirty. To do it sooner would interfere unduly with the town traffic. Nevertheless, it gives you only an hour to complete your cordon, Inspector Moll."

"An hour will be sufficient," said Inspector Moll. "It has been carefully rehearsed."

"I hope," said the Colonel, "that *everything* has been carefully rehearsed. The safety of a minister of state and a cardinal bishop is not a matter to be taken lightly. You all know the difficulties we have had with Italian troublemakers from the South Tyrol. I need hardly say that we want no incidents tomorrow. Not only the safety of the eminent persons but the honor of Lienz is in your hands." The thick lips parted in a smile. "I am certain it will be safe with you."

It was four o'clock before the door of the Franzkeller opened and Boschetto came out into the street. The grim mood of the morning was gone. The thick lips were parted in a smile. As he walked along the pavement he met and nodded to one or two acquaintances, who nodded cautiously in return.

In front of the post office in the main square he boarded the bus for Glaren, catching it as it was on the point of moving and booking a ticket to the terminus.

It is a forty-minute run from Lienz to Glaren, and Boschetto sat, his nose glued to the window, watching the mountains rising, high on both sides of the twisting road, but higher on the left than on the right as they approached the Italian border.

These were the Lienz Dolomites, the most beautiful but not the least formidable of the mountain ranges of Central Europe, looking their best that autumn afternoon. It was a landscape arranged vertically in four strips, each as sharply different as the colors on a hatband. First the hayfields, green after their last careful mowing, laced with little silver streams; above the pastures, the woodland, birch and pine and fir; above the woodlands, the rough uncultivated slopes, traversed by paths zigzagging between boulders and outcrop, seamed with ravines, a desolate buffer state; above that, the first snow of winter.

At the halt before Glaren, Boschetto got out, waiting beside the road until the bus had roared away, round a bend and out of sight. For the first time since he had left Lengberg prison that morning, a certain wariness seemed to have gripped him. He sat hunched on the bank beside the road and let three or four cars go by before hoisting himself to his feet and stepping up the track which left the road at this point and slanted up through orchard and pasture to the edge of the wood.

Once in the wood his movements became even more cautious. After a few yards he left the path and worked his way back through the undergrowth until he had reached a point where he could peer back down into the valley.

Below him, following side by side each twist in the valley floor, ran road, railway, and river. Ten miles ahead he could see the final twist in the valley where a shoulder of rock masked the road to Cortina and the Italian frontier.

He turned his attention to things nearer at hand: to the three men on bicycles who were pedaling laboriously up the road; to the two boys who were meant to be watching the cows in the meadow but were more intent on a small fire of sticks which they had built; to a man chopping wood on the edge of the woods immediately across the lateral valley ahead of him, the swing of his ax, the pause before the "clunk" followed in the still air.

A man came out of a cabin at the foot of the slope, below the point where the woodcutter was working. He was wearing a green coat, the uniform alike of the forest guards and the Grenzpolizei, or border police. Although the man was a full half mile away, Boschetto stiffened at the sight of him, then moved carefully back, farther into the bushes that concealed him.

The guard was smoking a pipe. He stared around him with the slow concentration of a man who is thinking of nothing much, waved to the woodcutter, who ignored him, and disappeared into the cabin.

It was a full five minutes before Boschetto stirred. Then he wriggled back through the undergrowth, reached the path, and started up it at a purposeful stride.

The path came out of the woods at a point where five ravines met, each running up at a different angle, splayed like the fingers of a hand. The palm of the hand was a tiny plateau, hidden from below by the woods and from above by the overhang of the hill.

Here Boschetto deserted the path, which went off to the right, following the contour, and selected the center ravine, which ran almost directly uphill. It was a narrow, winding cleft in the earth, formed by some glacial freak, its floor sprinkled with huge stones, its sides seamed with cracks. For perhaps a month in springtime, when the high snows melted, it would be a watercourse. For the rest of the year it was dry.

Boschetto was now going very slowly and seemed to be counting his paces. Once he hesitated and retraced his steps. Then he came on again. At a point where it was at its deepest, the ravine turned sharply round an outcrop of worn rock. Here Boschetto went on hands and knees and started to crawl.

With his body almost flat to the earth he moved

forward an inch at a time, past the base of the rock. He was scanning the ground with minute care. Once, and again, he paused, then moved on. Above his head the rays of the sun marched across, lengthening the shadows of rocks and trees, moving them almost perceptibly across the hillside. Down in the ravine it was already evening.

At last Boschetto saw what he was looking for. It was a stone, roughly square in shape and lighter in weight than the surrounding rock. He took out a knife, opened it, slid the big blade behind the edge of the stone and levered it out. Behind was a shallow cavity. In the cavity was a package, wrapped in oilskin, folded and refolded, and secured with black insulating tape.

Boschetto felt the weight of the package in the palm of his hand and smiled. It was safe. So much might have happened in three years. But no one had found it, no one had touched it.

He pushed the packet down inside his shirt and climbed the side of the ravine. He was moving more freely now and seemed to have lost some of his fear. As he came out onto the hillside, the long, level rays of the sun, shining directly across the valley, touched a splinter of reflected light. The reflection winked once and vanished.

A man who was not sharpsighted would not have noticed it. A careless man would have overlooked it. Boschetto was neither shortsighted nor careless. He knew that a pair of binoculars had been turned on him for a moment from the hillside opposite.

He started off at a lumbering run down the bare hillside, to ward the sheltering woods. As soon as he was among the trees he squatted down and tore open the package. First the insulating tape came off, strip after strip, then the outer covering of oilskin, then an inner covering. This was more difficult to deal with in haste and half-light, since the joins had been tamped down under a coating of grease. In the end Boschetto pulled out his knife again and sliced through the covering, pulling it off in strips in his eagerness to get at the contents.

First came a flat tin which had once held cocktail biscuits or something of the sort. It was full of Austrian and Italian currency: 500- and 1,000-schilling notes, and 5,000- and 10,000-lire notes, pressed together into a hard wad. These went, without further inspection, into Boschetto's pocket. The next item was an Italian passport, in a plastic case. This went into another pocket. The final object that Boschetto picked up and weighed lovingly in his hand was an automatic pistol. It was a Belgian Vorsicht, with the long barrel and the sliding sight. A marksman's gun, made with all the tender skill that the Brussels factory lavishes on its instruments of destruction.

Boschetto opened the front of his shirt and felt the gun drop down until it lay against his bare stomach. It felt hard and cold and heavy, and infinitely satisfying. His manhood was restored to him.

He bundled the tin and the wrappings together and pushed them under a bush. In all his preoccu-

14

pation he had not forgotten the telltale eye that had blinked at him. He had to move. But the darkness, which was now flowing, floodtide, into the valley, would help him.

He started off, traversing the woods, avoiding paths. His intention was to slip out at the farthest corner from his point of entry. Fortune was with him. The woods did not end abruptly, but straggled down into a fold of ground running toward the valley floor. If he kept in this he would have, at most, a hundred yards of meadow to cross before he came to the road, and once on the road his plans were made.

There was a ground mist lying in the meadow. Better still. Boschetto dropped onto his hands and knees and crawled forward. An unexpected obstacle loomed. It was a strong wire fence of six or seven strands. He scrambled over it and realized that he was on the railway line. He realized too that a train was coming. A fold in the hill had masked it, but now it came, swinging out of the gathering darkness, headlamps cutting a bright swath.

There was no time to climb back and nowhere to hide. Boschetto flattened himself against the wire.

It was a big, heavy train, with restaurant and sleeping cars. The lighted windows flicked past. The passengers, he was glad to see, were busy, reading, eating, and talking, lolling back in their seats, half asleep. Except for this one. Here was someone sitting upright staring straight out the window.

Boschetto was relieved to see that it was only a girl; English or American, he thought, in the brief glimpse he had of her face.

The last carriage passed him, and the red tail lamp swam steadily away into the mist and darkness.

2

Laura

THE DAY HAD STARTED AT FOUR O'CLOCK, in cold blackness, when the telephone beside Laura's bed had buzzed at her and the night porter had announced, with the complacent alertness of someone who has himself been up all night, that it was time for the signora to arise.

It would not have been so difficult if she had gone to bed sober and at a reasonable hour; but when you were twenty and in Rome for the first time, and had been looked after so well and so kindly, a last night meant a farewell party, and a farewell party, with Lorenz, meant a good deal to drink.

Laura sat on the edge of the bed wondering if she was going to be sick, and if so, whether she could reach the handbasin before it happened. Then she pulled herself together, walked quickly across, and started to brush her teeth. When in doubt or difficulty, brush your teeth.

Twenty minutes later she was down in the hall, packed and ready, her bill paid. Ten minutes later she was still packed, still ready, and still in the hall. The car, bespoken the night before, had not arrived.

The night porter shrugged his fashionably pointed shoulders. Things like that happened. Possibly the driver had mistaken the hour. Possibly he had gone to the wrong hotel. He must see if he could find a taxi, must he not? A further five minutes evaporated. Laura began to get worried. The Verona-Lienz express left Rome at ten minutes to five and it was not going to wait for her, not for a single second. If she missed it, there was no other train until midday, and that a slow one. It would mean changing her plans. It would mean telephoning her brother. It would mean saying hello to Lorenz, whom she had—well—almost finally said good-bye to the night before.

On the other hand, it would mean she could go back to bed.

At this point a screaming of worn brakes announced the arrival of the taxi.

She would have to tip the porter now. She knew exactly how much Italian money she had left. Two notes of a thousand lire and one of five hundred. Would five hundred lire be enough for such a majestic official as the night porter of the Hotel Maggiore, who had gone out, moreover, especially to get her a taxi? No. Better give him a thousand. A taxi ride to the station could hardly cost more than fifteen hundred lire.

In front of the gaunt concrete-and-glass façade of the Stazione Centrale she was undeceived.

"*What* did you say?"

"Tre mila."

"*Three* thousand?"

The small, black-haired driver with the urchin face held up three fingers and repeated, "Tre mila."

"But it's absurd," said Laura. "I never agreed to that." The long hand on the illuminated clock on the station front was nearing the three-quarter mark.

"I'll give you fifteen hundred—quindici cento —it's all I've got."

"Tre mila."

He no longer looked like an urchin. His face looked white, and ugly, under the neon lights.

"But that's nearly two pounds. It *can't* be two pounds to take me a quarter of a mile."

If I give him the money I've got, grab my suitcase and run, she thought . . . The driver, reading her thoughts, jumped down from his seat and scuttled round in front of her.

"Could I help?" asked a pleasant American voice.

She saw a young man carrying a battered suitcase.

"He's trying to charge me three thousand lire for taking me from the Hotel Maggiore," she said. "It's far too much—and anyway, I haven't got it."

"It's daylight robbery," said the young man.

"And I've got to get the ten-to-five train."

19

"So have I. How much have you got?"

"Fifteen hundred."

The young man said, "A thousand's quite enough." He took the note and gabbled something fluent-sounding in Italian. The only word Laura understood was "carabinieri." The taxi driver seemed to understand that too. Then the young man pushed the mille note into his hand, seized the suitcase, and took to his heels. Laura ran after him. They caught the train with one minute to spare.

As she rolled herself up in her coat and snuggled down into her reserved corner seat in an empty first-class carriage, determined to catch up with a few of the missing hours of sleep, Laura was plagued by a memory. Everything that had happened in the station square seemed to her to have happened before.

It was the situation. The girl, in a foreign country, getting into a situation, not of danger but of embarrassment, and being rescued from it by a resourceful young man. The stereotype of every woman's magazine. If she shut her eyes she could even see the picture, in four colors; it would occupy most of the lefthand side of the first page, an opening splash, after which the story, together with its hero and heroine, would dribble away into the obscurity of the advertisement columns, drying up, ultimately, a thin trickle of romance, lost in a desert of salesmanship.

Yet *had* he been resourceful? Had the driver, in fact, understood any of the fluent Italian that had washed over him or had he understood only that the young man meant business? If *she* had thrust a mille note at him, grabbed her suitcase, and run, would he have tried to stop her? Almost certainly not.

Ker-thud, ker-thud, ker-thud, said the train, gathering speed as it ran out of Rome and swung northeast along the banks of the Tiber.

He was an American. Americans always seemed to have their wits more about them than English people. They had more—more something or other—what was it?

The train whistled.

It was a succession of images that woke her. The train was running out of a tunnel, the light coming and going through slots in the tunnel wall, like a cinema film running off its spool. Her mouth was dry, and she felt as stiff as if she had spent a morning in the saddle.

It was after eight o'clock. There would be breakfast, if she could find it.

She made her way down the long succession of swaying corridors, past a German in shirt sleeves, unwashed and enjoying an early-morning cigar, past an Italian woman with three children waiting patiently for the lavatory door to open, past a party of students who had filled the corridor with a mountain of rucksacks and were sitting on it, looking as pleased as mountaineers on a peak.

In the restaurant car she found the young American. He waved to her and she came and sat down opposite him.

21

"I'm Joe Keller," he said without preamble. "From Galsworthy—that's in Pennsylvania, though I don't imagine you'd know that. It's not a very large place. Two thousand one-fifty at the last census."

If he'd just add his age and occupation, she thought, she'd have all the information necessary to fill out one of those little green cards they gave you in hotels.

"I work for a newspaper," he added.

Feeling that she was getting left behind, Laura said rapidly, "I'm Laura Hart. I'm just traveling abroad for fun. Well—not just for fun. It's a sort of convalescence."

"Nothing serious, I trust."

"I had my tonsils out. It doesn't *sound* bad, I know. But they were large tonsils. The surgeon who cut them out said they were the biggest he'd seen that year."

"What do you know?" said Mr. Keller. "I had mine out when I was four. My uncle—he was a medical student—did it for us, free. When he'd finished the tonsils, he got sort of enthusiastic and wanted to try his hand on my adenoids. I think he had ideas of tackling my freckles and pinning back my ears too. He was ahead of his time in plastic surgery. Where are you heading for?"

"I'm sorry?"

"Where are you going?"

"I'm going to Lienz."

"That's fine. So am I. We'll be able to see something of each other. Have you made reservations yet?"

"I didn't need to do that. I'm staying with my brother."

"Is he a resident?"

"No. Actually, he's vice-consul."

Joe Keller looked immediately impressed. "So your brother's in the Corps Diplomatique," he said. "I'd no idea."

"When you put it that way, it sounds a lot grander than it really is. Charles is only a vice-consul. That's almost the lowest thing you can be. He comes under the British Consul in Innsbruck, and *he's* under the Ambassador in Vienna. But I expect you know all that."

"I'm not intimately acquainted with the workings of your diplomatic service—or do you say consular service?"

"I believe they're both lumped together now, and called the foreign service."

"Is that so?"

She could see him making a mental note. Baseball, interplanetary missiles or love, he was a man who would like to get his technical terms right.

"What do you do?" she said. "Or are you traveling for pleasure too?"

"I haven't traveled strictly for pleasure since I was eighteen." He made it sound a long time ago. "I travel for business. My idea of a holiday is sitting still, and not catching trains or boats or airplanes."

"You're in business?"

"I'm a newspaperman. I move around looking for things to happen. When they start happening, I start sending cables."

"A special correspondent."

"Now it's my turn to be modest," said Joe Keller, looking anything but modest. "'Special correspondent' sounds like someone with an office, and contacts, and a big name. I haven't got any of those things."

"Not yet."

"You're too kind. What it is, I'm on a roving commission. I've got a nose for trouble. Or the editor of the *Mercury* thinks I have, which amounts to the same thing. The fact is, I had a piece of luck to start with, and that's what matters in the newspaper business. You remember what Napoleon said."

"He said such a lot of things."

"He said he liked lucky generals. It's the same with editors. They like you to be lucky. The first break I had, I was in South Africa, on a visit to my mother's family at North Point, when they had that little trouble at Sharpeville."

"*Little* trouble—" said Laura.

"That's all right," said Joe soothingly. "It upset me too. I thought it was terrible. But from the point of view of a newspaper with global coverage, to be in North Point, fifty miles from where it all happened, with good cable arrangements lined up—my mother's cousin was in the post office— you can see what it meant."

"I suppose so."

"Next thing I was in Algiers—nothing to do with politics. I was looking for one of our globe-trotting heiresses, who was said to have settled down there with a croupier from the casino, and bingo! I was right in the middle of the army revolt —not the second one, that fizzed—the first one. The one that really looked like getting somewhere."

"Imagine that," said Laura. She was trying to work out Joe's age. Suppose he'd been eighteen at the time of the Sharpeville massacre—how long ago *was* that? *She* had still been at school when it happened, and remembered adding her name to a round robin of protest, organized by the physics mistress, a curious little woman with red hair— what *was* her name?

"After three experiences like that," Joe was saying, "there was nothing else for it."

"I suppose not," said Laura. And to herself: *Three?* You've missed one, Laura. Keep your mind on the job.

"Lucky Joe, the editor called me. He used to tell the other boys, all you've got to do is watch where Joe plans to take his vacation. *Something's* bound to happen. A race riot. A plane crash. A revolution. I don't claim I was *responsible* for Castro. But like I said, I was in Cuba when he came along—"

"It can't all be luck," said Laura. "Not entirely. The first time, perhaps. But after that, I expect there was a good deal of judgment in it too."

"Maybe I have got a nose for trouble. Hello— what's he want?"

25

The conductor was hovering over them.

"Mr. Keller?"

"That's me."

"This cable's for you. It was handed in just as the train left. I regret we could not find you before."

"No harm," said Joe. "If I'd got it earlier there's nothing I could have done about it, is there?"

Laura was enthralled. She had once had luncheon with a businessman, a friend of her father's, who had received a telephone call from Paris during the second course, and the waiter had actually *placed the telephone on the table*, but to get a cable delivered to you on the Rome-Lienz express—

"I'd better go and decode this," said Joe. "The book's back in my compartment. I'll hope to see you at lunch."

In code, too.

At lunch Joe said, "It really is a coincidence, both of us going to Lienz. I bet you hadn't heard of it until your brother was posted there."

"I still muddled it up with Linz even after he'd been there for some time."

"I don't suppose one person in fifty could tell you, offhand. It's an important little place, though. And going to be more important still, if this trouble in the Tyrol develops."

"And is this the bit of trouble your—er—your nose is leading you to this time?"

The hitch, in the middle, was that she suddenly caught sight of his nose. It was not in the least the sort of nose one associated with keen investigators who got on the track of things: not long, not pointed, like Sherlock Holmes's. On the contrary, small and almost snub.

"That's right," said Joe. "That's the bit of trouble. Would it be a good idea if I bought a bottle of wine? Then you could share it with me."

"Well—"

"Fine. That's settled. The real trouble in the Tyrol is the Nazis."

She looked at him to see if he was serious. Apparently he was.

"Nazis? You mean Austrian Nazis?"

"I mean German Nazis. The old, true, dyed-in-the-wool, stamped-in-the-cork Heil-Hitler gang. Plenty of them left in Germany."

"But what have they got to do with the Tyrol?"

"Any sort of trouble's their business. They head for it like wasps for a jam jar. They don't wait to be asked. In fact, I should guess most of the Tyrolese hate their guts. But they couldn't pass up an opportunity like the Tyrol. It's their favorite sort of trouble—German speakers being oppressed by foreigners."

"*Are* the Italians oppressing them?"

"Depends on your point of view. The Italians say they're just governing them—maintaining law and order. The Germans say they're discriminating against them. And they don't like it, particularly since there are about twice as many Germans as Italians."

"If there are more Germans, why don't they let

them join Austria? I expect that's what they want to do, isn't it?"

"It isn't as simple as that."

"I bet it isn't," said Laura. "Politics never is. Tell me what's actually happening."

"The Germans are blowing up pylons and railways. The Italian federal police are trying to stop them. There's been quite a lot of shooting. Not many people have been killed yet, but there are one or two atrocity stories filtering out. Pretty ugly ones, lately."

"Atrocities by whom?"

"By the Italian police—on suspected terrorists or on innocent peasants, according to your point of view."

"What *is* this?"

"It's Chablis. A sort of white Burgundy, only a bit more so. Do you like it?"

"Yes. I do. How does Lienz come into it?"

"If you'd look at a map," said Joe, "you'd see the answer to that. See if I can explain." He laid knives and forks out on the table. "If you're coming south from Innsbruck, you come through North Tyrol as far as the Brenner. That's the gap between those two spoons. After that you're in South Tyrol—the Brenner's the Austrian-Italian border."

"And that's where all the trouble is?"

"Right. But if you go east from the Brenner— which you can't, because there are too many mountains in the way—but come a bit farther south, to Bixen—which the Italians call Bressanone—" he shifted a pepper pot—"and *then* go east, you'd get *back* into Austria. Austria sticks down a lot farther there. That's the new district of Lienz. O.K.?"

"O.K.," said Laura, "but what's special about it? Lots of countries jut out into other countries."

"What's special about it is this: Lienz is pretty well cut off from the rest of Austria. There are two ways in. One's up the Drava from Villach—that's not much of a road, and it doesn't really lead into the main part of Austria. The main road's from the north. That's over the Gross Glockner, one of the highest main roads in Europe. And it needs only one good fall of snow to block *that*. So most of the year an Innsbrucker who wants to get to Lienz goes over the Brenner—which *is* always open—and through Italy."

"And now he can't?"

"He can, but it's very much more difficult. When the trouble started, Italy imposed special visas and a lot of new restrictions, tightened up the customs formalities, and so on. If the situation gets worse, they may close the Brenner altogether. Then Lienz is out on a limb. That's why a few months back they handed them over a bit of autonomy. They control their own Landes police and security now, and have got a separate department for communications and another for light and power. Separate from Innsbruck, that is."

"It sounds as if they expect the Italians to start blowing up *their* pylons."

"I wouldn't know about that, but I can tell you

this, Miss Hart. It needs only one real incident, on either side of the frontier, and the situation could go up in smoke."

"Does your instinct suggest to you what's going to happen?" asked Laura. "Had you any particular sort of incident in mind?"

"Well," said Joe thoughtfully, "if they stopped blowing up pylons and blew up a trainful of passengers, now I'd call that an incident. Let me fill your glass."

"Thank you," said Laura.

When she got back to her carriage she found that the Chablis was combining against her with lack of sleep. She sank back into the corner. Outside, the autumn sunlight slanted across the Lombardy plain. Ahead, full in view now, stood the mountains. She was asleep before her chin had touched her chest.

The Austrian customs official who boarded the train at Cortina was a kindhearted man. He looked at the girl sleeping in the corner, looked at the labels on her luggage, and said to his Italian colleague, "She is British."

"Evidently," said the Italian.

"Then she will have a British passport."

"Inevitably."

They let her sleep on.

It was evening before she stirred, remembered where she was, stretched, and looked out the window.

They were running down a long, narrow valley, a cleft in the mountains holding railway, road, and river. Where they were the sun had set, but it was still crimsoning the high tops and casting a reflected glow into the valley. From the stream an evening mist was billowing up, creeping over the meadows, blanketing the road.

A man was standing beside the track, just inside the boundary wire. She had the illusion that he was looking straight at her.

3

Dinner with
the Hofrat

LIENZ, THAT EVENING, was looking charming. There is a moment in late autumn when á strong magic grips the Tyrol. The countryside is waiting, swept and garnished, for the arrival of winter. Day after day the winds blow gently from the south, the skies are blue, the sun is benevolently warm. On the high tops the first snow has fallen and lies remote and unmenacing, the warmth that rises from the valleys distilling a fringe of mist along its lower edge. The Austrians enjoy it, but warily. They know that one morning, suddenly, they will wake to find the skies dull gray. The wind will have swung to the north and will be piloting in a convoy of clouds, drab as dirty cotton wool. *Bald Kommt der Schnee.*

It was the last of a week of such days, the ultimate fling of autumn. Laura left her brother's flat after tea. After a good night's rest, breakfast in bed, and a leisurely morning of shopping and sightseeing, she felt ready for anything life might offer.

"I'm afraid you're going to have rather a crowded program," her brother had said before departing for the consulate. "We've got the Hofrat coming to dinner. He accepted the invitation some time ago, though I fancy he'd like to get out of it now. He's got a lot on his hands. Bundesminister Franz Miller—roughly the equivalent of our Home Secretary—is coming here from Vienna tomorrow, bringing a cardinal bishop with him— he's a local boy from the Tyrol. The militia's turning out in force—the Bishop is going to bless a new set of colors that Miller will present to them. It'll be the biggest show they've had in Lienz for years. Several awkward questions of protocol, though."

Absurd, thought Laura, to hear Charles talking about awkward questions of protocol, when it seemed only yesterday that he was trying to slink into meals without washing, a tactic doomed to failure with their sharp-eyed mother.

No. Not yesterday. The day before yesterday. There had been an interval when all contact had been lost. She at school, and then in Lausanne. Charles at Oxford, and in Athens. Now, half kin, half strangers, they were meeting again.

"Is it the sort of dinner one dresses for?"

"I shall wear a dinner jacket."

"Would a cocktail dress do?"

"It sounds most appropriate. Frau Rosa will look after you. She doesn't speak much English, but if you take it slowly she'll understand you. I shan't be back until after tea. You're sure you'll be all right?"

"I shall be fine," said Laura. "Don't you worry about me. I'm going for a walk this afternoon."

"Don't go wandering off into the mountains."

"I wasn't intending to wander any farther than the nearest shopping center," said Laura. "What's wrong with the mountains, anyway?"

"I've never really found out, but a regular succession of people, mostly English, go out for walks on the mountains here and don't come back."

"What happens to them?"

"They are usually *found*," said her brother, "at the bottom of precipices."

Frau Rosa, in slow and careful German, had delivered a similar warning. The upper slopes of the mountains, below the snow line, were places of danger.

"What sort of danger?" asked Laura. But Frau Rosa either misunderstood the question or decided to evade it. "The mountains are very beautiful," she said, "when one views them from below."

Laura spent a fascinating afternoon. She wandered through ancient courts and alleyways. She ventured into the incense-smelling gloom of the Hofkirche and peered at the finest monumental sarcophagus in Western Europe. She penetrated a huge, barnlike shop which had uncut hides hanging from wooden racks and was presided over by the largest woman she had ever seen outside a circus, who smoked and coughed alternately and sold her a beautiful leather handbag. She had tea in the Hofgarten, and sat for a long time listening to the band. There were three men, in bottle-green uniforms with orange facings, playing identical brass instruments, complex affairs of tube, cylinder, and slide. Two looked mournful and one cheerful. All of them had beards.

The sun touched the mountaintop, the shadows lengthened, and Laura discovered, to her surprise, that the afternoon had gone. It was nearly seven o'clock.

She attracted the attention of a scurrying waiter, paid her bill, and started to make her way back. She had no fear of losing herself. Her brother's flat was near the main railway station, on the other side of the town. All she had to do was to keep the railway on her right and the river on her left and she could not go wrong.

As a strategic plan it was sound. Like many strategic plans, it fell down on small points of tactics. Faced with a choice of two streets, neither of which really led in the right direction, she selected one at random, and soon got the impression that it was bearing too far to the left; much too far.

She had decided to turn around and try again when a promising alleyway opened up on the right. She turned down it. It was narrow, cobbled, and dark. In one wall there showed an occasional tightly shuttered window. The other wall was blank.

If it gets much narrower, she thought, I shall have to progress sideways. This is stupid. It must come out somewhere. Irritatingly, it turned once more in the wrong direction. But as she rounded the turn she saw an arched entrance ahead, leading into what looked like an open space.

At that moment, somewhere in front of her, she heard footsteps, running. First came one set of lighter steps. Then a lot of heavier steps, in pursuit. As she reached the mouth of the alley she saw the end of the chase.

The pursuers were three young men in the local dress of wide, leather-cuffed trousers and blouse-like shirts. The quarry was a man in his middle twenties, with black hair and olive skin.

Realizing that he had run into an impasse, he was now standing with his back to the wall, staring at his pursuers. They had spread across the street and were advancing, slowly, now that they were sure of their kill.

One of them said something. His accent, had she been expert enough to realize it, did not match his Tyrolese dress. When they were nearly up to him the black-haired man made a jump for freedom, pushing past the leader of the trio. It was a futile gesture. The other two caught him by an arm each, and twisted the arm up behind the man's back with such force that he screamed.

Up to this moment Laura had thought the whole thing might have been a joke, a piece of apprentices' horseplay. Now she realized, with a feeling of sickness, that they meant business. The three of them were going to hurt the fourth man, deliberately, and for their own ends. It was not kindersport.

She was in the mouth of the alleyway, hidden

by a buttress. The three men were not more than a few yards away, across the street. As she watched, the one who seemed to be the leader, and who looked the youngest, drew his hand back and smacked the black-haired man across the face. It was more than a smack. It was a punch, delivered with the hand open. It caught the black-haired man full across the cheek and nose, and jerked his face round. The second blow came from the left hand. Laura caught the gleam of a gold ring. As the blow landed, with great force, the black-haired man started to scream.

She found herself running forward.

"Stop it," she said. "Stop it, at once, do you hear?"

The leader turned slowly. She could see him more clearly now. It was a striking face. Pretty, she thought, almost girlish. A thin straight nose, a generous mouth, and blond hair slicked back. Light-blue eyes. He was smiling, and seemed untroubled by the fact that he had a witness.

"You are English?" he said. He spoke reasonable English himself.

"Yes, I'm English. Let him alone."

He looked her up and down.

"Would you like to see him dance?" He turned to the man. "Dance for the lady, Italian monkey. Dance on your barrel organ."

Raising his boot, he stamped heavily on the Italian's foot. The Italian screamed again.

One of the men said something. The fair-haired leader turned to Laura.

"My friend suggests that he would dance better without his trousers. Have you ever seen an Italian without his trousers? It is a formidable sight."

All three roared with laughter, and one of the men smacked the Italian in the stomach, doubling him up.

"Even Giuseppe laughs," said the leader. "See how he laughs? He cannot stand upright for laughter."

"I shall fetch the police," said Laura. She was trembling so much that the words would scarcely come out. As she turned and ran, the laughter boomed behind her down the courtyard, followed by the thud of another blow and a thin and bloodless whimpering.

She found a policeman at the corner of the next street where it turned into one of the main shopping centers. She was out of breath, and shaking. It took some minutes of her patient and limited German to tell him what she wanted. Then he swung ponderously round and moved off down the street, without waiting to see if she followed.

The court, as she had guessed it would be, was empty.

"Boys," said the policeman.

"They were *not* boys," she said. For God's sake, why can't I speak German properly? How can I explain, in schoolgirl sentences of elementary words without a verb, that an atrocity has been committed within fifty yards of where he was standing? A small atrocity, perhaps, but all atrocities started as bullying and bearbaiting. That was the time to stop them, before the state took over the apparatus of bully or counterbully, with underground room and leather strap and steel hook.

"You were assaulted?"

"Nobody touched me," she said.

"You have a complaint, then?"

"I have no complaint, but I think you ought to do something about it."

She saw, by his look of blank incomprehension, that she was getting nowhere.

"I am sorry," she said. "They have all gone now. It is nothing."

He smiled paternally. "You were frightened," he said. "They are rough boys, but they mean no real harm. What hotel are you staying at?"

"No hotel. I am staying with my brother. He is British Vice-Consul in Lienz."

This appeared to make some impression on the policeman. If the woman was not simply a tourist, if she had some official standing, it was possible— just possible—that her story would have to be investigated.

"Would you wish," he said, "to come to the police headquarters and to make a statement?"

"No," said Laura. Her mind was made up. "I have no statement to make."

"You are quite sure?"

"Yes, quite sure."

"Allow me, then, to show you your way back to the consulate."

*   *   *

"You have chosen the right moment to visit the Tyrol," said Hofrat Humbold. "In Lienz we call this Bellermanswoch. The Bellerman is the old man who goes round after the feast is over, cleaning up the tables and snuffing the candles."

He said this in the dry tones of a schoolmaster leading his class over well-worn tracks of exposition. He had a prim mouth, gold spectacles, hair running back in a neat fan from a point in the center of his forehead. She could picture him in some small country schoolhouse, on a somnolent afternoon, rapping with his pointer on his raised desk to keep the sleepy children attentive.

"But when the Bellerman has finished his work, when he has extinguished the last candle, the snow will come."

"I hope I shall still be here," said Laura. "I love the snow."

"You are a skier?" This was from the fourth member of the dinner party. Describing him, Charles had said, "Helmut Angel. In England or America I suppose he'd be called a playboy, but on the Continent a young man seems to be allowed to live on the money his father has accumulated without attracting derogatory descriptions. He's a good climber. He was one of the four men who went up the north face of the Wetterstein last year. He drives a French Facel Vega very fast indeed, and he has a chance of being in the Austrian team for the International Winter Sports."

Upon which she had said, "You're not trying to put me off him, by any chance?"

But Helmut had confounded her. He was far from good-looking. He was chunky. He looked as if the Creator had put him together in an absent-minded mood, had then rather liked the finished product, and had carefully sandpapered off the rougher pieces, without being able to disguise the fact that the basic blueprint was misconceived. His face was certainly brown but could scarcely have been described as bronzed. It was brown in the way that a very old portmanteau is brown. The nose was wide, the mouth big, but not full, and there was positively and unmistakably a dimple in the middle of the rounded chin.

"I have skied a little," she said. "I like it, but I fall down a good deal."

"Everyone falls down," said Helmut. "I once fell, head downward, into a crevasse, and hung there, supported only by my skis."

"I thought that happened only in comic papers, like getting hitched up on punt poles."

"There was nothing comic about this, I assure you. I hung there for more than an hour."

"How did you get out?"

"I decided, in the end, that I should either hang there until I froze, or I must fall into the crevasse. The second seemed the better alternative. I succeeded in wriggling out of the boot straps, and fell. Fortunately I landed on a ledge not too far down. Then I climbed out. It was a lesson."

"A lesson?"

"A lesson not to go into the mountains alone. In the mountains you meet a host of enemies. Loose snow, brittle ice, strong winds, cold, vertigo. It is stupid to add loneliness to them as well. I prefer, now, to go with two or three companions."

"You're the third person today who has warned me against the mountains. Both my brother and his housekeeper seemed to think that I should wander off into them, and never be seen again."

Humbold had been following this conversation closely, rotating his head toward each speaker in turn.

He said, "You should not disregard the warning, Miss Hart. There are wild men in the mountains. They live in caves and holes in the mountainside, like beasts. Occasionally we have a drive to clear them out. But it is difficult. They live close to the frontier, and have only to cross it to be safe. Many of them *are* Italians."

"There was that woman tourist, only last February," said Helmut. "The one they found under a rock—but I apologize." He caught Charles's eye on him. "It is not a very pleasant conversation for the dinner table."

"How are your preparations going forward for tomorrow, Herr Humbold?" asked Charles.

"Our preparations are complete."

"Do you anticipate trouble?"

"There will inevitably be trouble. Trouble with crowds coming to and from the square. Trouble with traffic. Trouble with the extra security measures we shall have to impose."

"I suppose so, yes."

"We are a new state. I feel that we are on trial in

this matter. The safety of a Bundesminister and a cardinal bishop has been entrusted to us. It is a heavy responsibility."

Laura had a clear vision of Miss Sennett, her late headmistress. "Tomorrow we are expecting Lord Penticost, our chairman of governors. Every girl is on her honor to uphold the good name and traditions of this school—"

"By trouble," said Charles, "I really meant racial trouble. I couldn't help noticing a slight increase of rowdiness—slogans printed on walls, that sort of thing."

"There is a subversive Italian element in Lienz. It is small, but troublesome. I have sometimes suspected that it receives support from our political opponents."

"Political opponents will always fish in troubled waters," agreed Charles. "Had you anyone particular in mind?"

"Radler had an Italian grandmother."

"Ernst Radler? The Socialist leader? Surely he would not lend himself—"

"A man who will not lend himself will sometimes sell himself," said Humbold.

"Surely, you don't suggest—"

"Not for money, no. But for power. There are men to whom power is more precious than money."

"In my book, then, they're mad," said Helmut. "Money brings pleasure. Power brings headaches."

Laura said, "Have you *really* got a troublesome Italian minority here?"

Humbold swiveled his head round and awarded her one of Miss Sennett's most transfixing glances.

"What do you mean, Miss Hart?"

I won't be intimidated, said Laura to herself. This is my brother's dinner table. Technically I'm on British territory. I am *not* a small girl. "I meant," she said carefully, "that national minorities sometimes get blamed for a lot of trouble that has nothing to do with them."

"Really, Laura—" said Charles.

"They form a sort of useful whipping boy."

"Or scapegoat," suggested Helmut.

"How long have you been in Lienz, Miss Hart?"

Laura looked at her watch. "Exactly twenty-six hours."

"Then I must suggest that people who have been studying the problem for a quarter of a century would be likely to have a more balanced view of it."

She glimpsed, on one side, Charles frowning and caught, on the other, a flash of encouragement from Helmut.

"We have a saying," she said, "that it is sometimes difficult to see the woods for the trees."

"And what does it mean?"

"Well—" What *did* it mean? "It implies that if you get too immersed in a problem you might, conceivably, find it difficult to take an over-all view of what is going on."

"The spectator," said Helmut, "sees most of the game. Yes?"

Humbold transferred his attention briefly to

Helmut, who smiled at him, and then turned back to Laura.

"And in your twenty-six hours of being a spectator of our national game you have come to the conclusion that we have not got a troublesome Italian minority."

"I didn't quite mean that," said Laura. "But it occurred to me that the Italians might be having their own troubles too."

"And when did this thought come into your mind, Miss Hart?"

"About an hour ago when I happened to see an Italian being beaten up by three Austrians."

She described the incident.

"Did you report the incident, Miss Hart?"

"I told the first policeman I saw."

"His name?"

"I don't know his name."

"Surely, when you were at the police station, making a statement, you discovered his name."

"I didn't go to the police station. And I didn't make a statement."

"Why not?"

"I—"

"It was, as you describe it, a serious assault. A criminal assault. Surely it was your duty, as a witness, to make a statement."

Laura felt herself getting hot. Charles was silent. His expression said, "You've got yourself into this. You can get yourself out of it."

"The policeman," she said, "didn't seem to want to take it very seriously."

"He discouraged you from making a statement?"

"No, I wouldn't say that."

"Did he invite you to make one?"

"Yes—as a matter of fact he did."

"And you refused."

"He said it was probably apprentices or students. He evidently thought I was exaggerating."

"Yes," said Humbold.

"Coffee in the next room," said Charles hastily.

4

The Bishop Speaks

"REALLY, LAURA," said Charles.

"I can see I'm not cut out to be a diplomat," said Laura, "but you must admit he provoked me."

Herr Humbold had left on the stroke of ten. After his departure the atmosphere had lightened. Helmut had accepted another glass of brandy and had proceeded to entertain them with stories of motor racing and the International Winter Sports set. At eleven o'clock he, too, had gone, leaving brother and sister together.

"I thought *you* provoked *him*."

"It wasn't what he said. It was just that he reminded me of Miss Sennett."

"Miss who?"

"The headmistress at Highside."

"Really, Laura."

"He pursed his lips in exactly the same way that she did. And he treated me as if I was a child."

"He's got a lot on his mind just now."

"Such as what?"

"Well, there really has been trouble over the South Tyrol. It's not imaginary. And it could turn quite nasty."

"What I don't understand is, just who's making the trouble. South Tyrol belongs to the Italians. Yes?"

"It doesn't belong to them. It was awarded to them, after the First World War. They were on our side in that war."

"But they were against us this time. So why didn't they have to give it back?"

"The only people they could have given it back to was the Austrians. They were on the losing side too."

"I think it's horrible," said Laura, "trading countries across the table as if they were counters. Why don't they ask the people who live there? They're the ones who should decide."

"A plebiscite?"

"Why not?"

"If they had a plebiscite of Bolzano Province— which is the one most of the argument is about—I can tell you exactly what the result would be. A two-to-one vote for coming back to Austria."

"All right, then—"

"On the other hand, the Italians say that Bolzano shouldn't be considered by itself. They would be quite prepared to have a plebiscite of the whole of the Region—that's Bolzano *and* Trento."

"Because there are enough Italians in Trento to swing the vote the other way."

"Quite right."

"The whole thing's a swindle," said Laura. "The only answer is to make them completely independent. Like Switzerland. I'm going to bed."

She added, as she made for the door, "I suppose there's no truth in the rumor that the trouble's being stirred up by ex-Nazis?"

For the first time a ripple broke the surface of Charles's diplomatic calm.

"I don't think so," he said. "Who put that idea into your head?"

"An American called Joe," said Laura. "I met him on the train. He has an infallible nose for trouble. He told me so himself."

"Going to the parade, Miss Hart?"

"Oh, it's you, Mr. Keller. Yes, I'm meeting my brother there."

"Join me in a cup of coffee first."

"I'd love to," said Laura. "But do you think we ought? It's due to start at eleven o'clock and it's five to now."

"It's a full-dress military shebang. There'll be half an hour of forming line and marching and countermarching before business begins. You've got a ticket for the VIP seats, I suppose."

"Row C. Wives and Ladies of the Diplomatic Corps."

"That's all right then. Plenty of time for a coffee. Let's sit outside. Make the most of this sun while it lasts."

As they took their seats, a stocky figure got up

from one of the far tables and ambled across. It was Helmut. His brown face crinkled into a smile as he recognized Laura.

"I shall see you at the parade?" he said.

"Certainly."

"The speeches will be dull for you, but it will be a fine spectacle."

They watched him cross the pavement and get into the low-slung scarlet Facel Vega.

"I've a feeling I know that guy," said Joe.

"Helmut Angel."

"That's right. Of course. Mountain climbing, ski jumping, racing cars. All the really expensive ways of breaking your neck."

"If you've got a lot of money to spend, that sounds quite a—well, quite a healthy way of spending it."

Joe looked at her thoughtfully, and then said, "Oh, sure. Sure. A great boy. He's interested in politics too, I'm told."

"What sort of politics?"

"Does the Tiroler Boden Bund mean anything to you? Or the name Berg Isel?"

"Nothing at all. I don't even know who Berg Isel is."

"Oh, Fame, oh, Fame, how short thy span! Short as the Memory of Man! Berg Isel was a battle. It was one of the greatest victories ever gained by irregular troops over a regular army. It's a place near Innsbruck—a sort of tea garden now—where Andreas Hofer, of blessed memory, routed the Bavarian troops."

"Is he the gentleman with the beard that they've got all the statues of?"

"That's him."

"And when did it all happen?"

"A hundred and fifty years ago—just about."

"Oh, well," said Laura. "You couldn't expect me to know about a thing like that."

"People around here know about it," said Joe. "They've got long memories in these parts. Whenever something happens which they regard as a threat to the Tyrol—the historic Tyrol—Andreas Hofer burnishes up his arms—and people like your friend Helmut join the Berg Isel Bund, which is fairly respectable, or the Tiroler Boden Bund, which is definitely fanatical."

"He's not my friend," said Laura. "I've met him precisely once, at dinner last night. All the same, I could hardly help liking him. He was such a pleasant contrast to our other guest."

Joe paused for a moment in his endeavor to attract the attention of the elderly waiter and said, "Who was he?"

"Herr Humbold."

"The Hofrat?"

"That's right."

"Well now," said Joe. "What I wouldn't have given to be there. That's a man who's come a long way in a short time."

"And knows it."

"Right, I've heard that modesty's not his strong suit. But you've got to admit, he's got something to buck about. At the end of the war he was an unsuccessful dentist in Vienna. Five years later he was a deputy. He was undersecretary for agriculture in the first Christian Democrat government, and minister of health in the second. Then the idea got about that he'd cast himself as prime minister in the next government. He was busy drumming up a coalition of all the parties of the Center with an anti-Socialist program—"

"He doesn't seem to like the Socialists," agreed Laura.

"He's a politician," said Joe. She wasn't sure from his tone of voice whether this was an excuse or an explanation.

"How did he get to Lienz?"

"It's an old rule of politics. When a subordinate gets ambitious, you send him off to rule a distant province. The Romans thought that one up. Sometimes it works all right. Out of sight out of mind. Sometimes it backfires. The proconsul gets up such a head of steam in his own province that it blows him back into power in the capital."

"He didn't strike me as the sort of man who would be likely to make a mark in history. He wasn't—" having got that far she could hardly say that her views on him were colored by his resemblance to her late headmistress— "he wasn't a big enough sort of man," she concluded rather lamely.

"Most of the trouble in this world," said Joe, "has been caused by small men. Napoleon was five feet two. Hitler was five feet three. If that goddam expert in slow motion who's disguised as a waiter doesn't hurry with the check, we shall miss the parade."

It took them five minutes to push their way through the thickening crowd, sightseers rather than spectators, which had gathered round the approaches to the square, attracted by the Tyrolese band, which was in full blast. Once inside the square they ran into a more serious obstacle in the form of a cordon of auxiliary police. Unlike English policemen, Laura noted, they were facing the crowd they were intended to restrain, and had the particularly expressionless appearance of civilians suddenly called on to perform an official function. Joe selected the most sympathetic looking, and showed him his pass. The man shook his head. "But look here," said Joe. "We've got to get in. This is a press pass. Newspapers. You understand."

"It is too late to pass."

"It's not too late. The parade hasn't started yet. That's just the overture. Look here, try *your* pass on him."

Laura produced her invitation. It was an impressive document, inviting Laura to take her seat in the places reserved for guests of the Diplomatic Corps, and it was topped by a large red bird, either a dove or an eagle, or a heraldic hybrid of both. The policeman showed signs of weakening and summoned an officer.

A foxy-faced man introduced himself as Inspector Moll.

"I will show you to the reserved section," he

said. "It would have been better had you arrived at eleven o'clock."

"I'm terribly sorry," said Laura.

"It's quite an organization you've got going here," said Joe. "I've been to parades all over the world, but I've never seen such a security turnout. Are you expecting trouble?"

"You are with this lady?"

"I happen to be an acquaintance of this lady. I'm not with her. I'm here on a press ticket."

"There is a section reserved for newspaper reporters. It is between the Andreas Hofer memorial and the public convenience."

One by one the soldiers in their dark-green uniforms raised their hands; one by one they gave a strangled shout which Laura took to be their declaration of loyalty to their new colors. With an English regiment the ceremonial would have seemed ridiculous; with these people, in that setting, it suddenly became impressive. She remembered her brother's saying, "If the Russians march into Europe we shall have one front line on the Alps and another on the Pyrenees." These men would fight on the Alps.

The band struck up the Tyrolese national anthem, the "Landeshymne." The long pennants rippled on the flagstaffs. The sun shone out of a pale-blue sky. It was a perfect setting for the ceremonial.

The two wings of the stage were the old Imperial Palace, the long frontage of which formed the left-hand side of the square; and the State Theater, on the steps of which the dignitaries were standing.

The back cloth was the mountains; a symphony of color, form, and movement which would have baffled a painter but might have inspired a musician.

The spectators reseated themselves, and the first guest of honor rose to the microphone.

Bundesminister Miller was a tall, thin, dry man who might have stepped from a board room in any capital city of the Western world. He was well but unemphatically dressed. His face was not exactly expressionless. It possessed, rather, a number of well-organized expressions, each one suitable for a specific occasion.

Laura was unable to understand anything that he said, but she did realize that he was failing to grip his audience.

The official guests sat in attitudes of polite attention, but those Lienzers who had reached the square early enough to take up a position inside the cordon, and who formed a sort of bright inner circle round the lines of chairs, were beginning to stir and chatter gently among themselves. Feet began to shift, heads were turned. The politically balanced thesis and antithesis of Dr. Miller, previously drafted and agreed upon with his Cabinet colleagues, laid on a dozen editorial desks, cut and dried to a point where words meant anything that you wished them to mean, or nothing at all, drifted like thistledown over the holiday crowd. Laura transferred her attention to the theater. It was an ugly but striking building. Builders of theaters, she reflected, having to be economical within, usually let themselves go when it comes to exteriors. This one was no exception.

It had a massive portico, supported by three Doric columns on each side. It had two shallow flights of steps, separated by a spacious platform on which the official guests were now seated. Deserting the classical idiom, the architect had then added, at either side of the portico, a turret of a type commoner in grand opera than in life, topped by a machicolated roof and pierced by three circular windows, one above the other. The façade was coated with plaster, painted light yellow and flaking in places.

Dr. Miller reached his peroration, worked himself into a carefully regulated outburst of fury, blew his nose, ceased being furious, and sat down. Hofrat Humbold, who was seated beside him, smiled, and the guests applauded politely. At a signal from the master of ceremonies the band struck up a brisk marching tune and Laura imagined that this was the signal for dispersal. However, she noticed that no one seemed to be moving, and when the marching tune finished the crowd had lost its restlessness. Even the noisiest group, which she had observed clustered around a lamp standard immediately in front of her, had fallen silent and attentive.

"Ausprache," she read on her program, "des Militärvikar Sc: Eminenz Kardinal Bischof Hubert." And as she looked up again the Bishop was rising to his feet.

The first surprise was that he was not an old man. The lines of austerity and self-will cut into his pale face made it difficult to judge accurately, but he was a man, she thought, of no more than fifty. The nose was thin and straight; the mouth an uncompromising slit. From under thick eyebrows a pair of burning eyes looked out at a world of lesser men. Here was no holy dotard. Here was a fighter. A man who had discarded the easy shield of compromise and tact and soft dealing; a man who, when he hit his enemies, intended to hurt them.

At his first few words a low murmuring ran through the crowd. Laura, who had been brought up almost inside a hunt kennels, thought of hounds. The quarry was not in sight but a hint, a faint and illusive hint, of his presence had reached the keener noses of the pack.

And in some curious way, and still without understanding more than isolated words, she knew what he was saying. He was speaking of the glories of "Heiliges Land Tirol"; of the traditions of the hardy mountain folk who lived there, a small, but very precious, fragment of the human family, isolated, in difficulties, alone—betrayed. Betrayed. She felt certain he had used that word, and as he spoke it the crowd broke into a deep, baying roar of applause.

Laura looked at the platform. On one side of the Bishop, Dr. Miller sat, impassive. On the other, Hofrat Humbold was stirring. He cast a glance, first toward the crowd, then at the other distinguished guests, a chief secretary from Vienna, the honorary colonel of the regiment, and a number of other people whose functions she could only dimly guess.

The Diplomatic Corps was concentrating with the painful attention of men who would have to summarize and pass on to their superiors, in Paris, Berlin, London and The Hague, every word that was now being spoken.

Laura's attention was again attracted to the crowd. It was undoubtedly enthusiastic, but it was not entirely unanimous. References to the virtues and sufferings of the Tyrolese were applauded, but when the speaker, his eyes burning in his white face, turned his artillery on the oppressors, when he spoke—and she could hear the venom in his voice—of the "Joch der Italiener" she could sense a restlessness in some parts of the crowd.

The group that she had noticed before, standing under the lamppost immediately opposite to her, appeared to be conducting a private debate in counterpoint to the Bishop's speech.

She looked at them more closely. There were four or five men, the most noticeable of whom was a tall, black-haired character in the middle who had his back to the speaker and appeared to be haranguing the group. A smaller man had hold of his left arm and the rest were either restraining him or egging him on. Behind them the crowd swayed in sympathy. It was as if in a deep, strong-flowing current a movement of opposition had made itself felt. There was a center of turbulence, tiny as yet but significant.

The Bishop stood for a few seconds without speaking. It was Merlin, brooding over the spirits he had raised; an unforgettable figure, tall, aesthetic, and mischievous, a pillar of ivory topped by the scarlet flame of a cardinal's hat.

The eyes of every man and woman in the crowd were fixed on him; except Laura's. She was looking at a point above and to the right of the Bishop. There, as she had noticed before, was a circular window in one of the turrets that flanked the portico. When she had first looked at it she had imagined that it was a fixed window, but she saw that this was not so. The top half, a semicircle of frosted glass in an iron frame, opened outward on a ratchet. And it was opening now, slowly but quite steadily. And through the opening something protruded, something dull black, which gave back a glint of metal.

A voice shouted from the group in front of her. It was the tall black-haired man, who was tearing himself free from his neighbors and was waving his arm and shouting. Women screamed.

Laura's eyes were on the black gun barrel protruding from the window. She saw it jump once, twice, as the shots came.

The Bishop swung round in a violent gesture. It was as if he turned to face an interruption from an unexpected source. Then he went down onto his knees, and pitched slowly forward onto his face. His scarlet hat tumbled from his head and rolled down the shallow steps.

5

The Last of the
Fine Weather

Laura was one of the first to move. Jumping
to her feet, she kicked her chair over and started
out at a stumbling run toward the section where
the Diplomatic Corps was seated. Her one idea
was to get close to Charles.

Then the paralysis of affront and shock snapped
like an overtight string. There was a roar as the
crowd surged forward, in an unreasoning reaction,
a desire to move, to stamp, to grab. It was the
instinct of a huge animal, wounded in one of its
extremities, rolling and threshing.

The ropes that separated the standing crowd
from the seats burst, seats went over as the audience jumped up, there was a smashing of wood,
and a wave of bodies lapped up against the steps of
the theater. Above the roar of the crowd rose the
steady screaming of women.

Laura missed Charles but reached the steps and
found shelter behind one of the pillars. She looked

down at the square. It was as though a gust of hurricane force had picked up a section of the crowd and thrown it against the steps. But in that forward surge there were already two countermovements. At one point, under the lamppost, a private war was being waged. She glimpsed the tall, black-haired man, his arms flailing, shot up for a moment like a log in a millrace, then submerged under the bodies of his attackers.

In the middle of the crowd, directly opposite the steps, another and stronger movement was developing. The troops were coming in; small but determined men in green, butting, pushing and boring. As she watched, the head of the column reached the front of the steps, the officer in charge shouted, and the men turned outward, forming a cordon.

Overhead a loudspeaker crackled and boomed, and a voice started giving orders.

Laura found Charles beside her. His black Homburg hat was over one eye, but he looked comfortingly matter-of-fact.

"I think you'd better get back to the flat," he said. "There's still a way out behind the theater, if you jump to it."

"Charles, I saw it—"

"We all saw it," said Charles. "It was a bestial thing. They've got the man, that's one comfort. I expect they've torn him to pieces by now."

"But, Charles—"

"It was that tall black-haired man under the lamppost. I caught a glimpse of him as he fired.

62

He looked like an Italian. There's going to be trouble if he was."

She opened her mouth to say something, but Charles was already hustling her across the steps and down the side of the theater. There was a hooped-iron fence, shoulder high.

"I'll give you a leg up," he said. "See if you can work your way round to the back of the theater. The crowd isn't right round yet. I've got to get back."

Laura ran along the strip of lawn. The crowd, packed against the outside of the fence, had no eyes for her. They were craning and pressing toward the square, infected by a common excitement but uncertain of what had happened.

Ahead of Laura was a second fence, flanking a path leading to one of the side doors of the theater. She was actually climbing the fence when the door opened and someone came out. It was the pretty, blond-haired boy she had seen the night before attacking the Italian. And, as she was immediately and completely certain, it was the murderer of the Bishop.

It was this certainty, which had no basis in logic but was the stronger for being illogical, that made her scream.

The boy looked at her, and for a second she saw in his eyes a mixture of alarm and hatred that turned her blood cold. Then he turned on his heel, ran the few yards to the end of the path, and started to shoulder his way through the crowd.

She found herself running after him, shouting

"Stop him! Murderer!" Faces turned and looked blankly at her. Then she was herself in the crowd. A man grabbed her. She shook herself loose, hitting him in the face as she did so. Behind her someone growled out something. The boy was well ahead of her now, working his way through the crowd. As she tried to push after him a foot came out and tripped her. She went down on her knees. Two hands came down, grabbed her arms, and hauled her to her feet.

"Better get out of here before they start getting rough," said the voice of Helmut.

He kept hold of her wrists and started to back out, pulling her after him in a series of jerks. People were shouting. A face looked down at her, stupid with fear and excitement. A hand grabbed her dress near the shoulder, and she heard the tearing noise as the stuff went. The next moment they were clear.

"No need to run," said Helmut. "They won't chase you. They just didn't like you treading on their toes. They're a bit worked up."

They walked down one of the passages at the rear of the theater and came out into a street of shops. Behind them they could hear the roar of the crowd, dominated by the booming of the loudspeaker.

She said, "Would you mind stopping for a moment? I can't—"

She was trembling so violently that she couldn't speak.

Helmut put an arm under hers and steered her

through a doorway. She found herself seated at a table.

"What you need is a drink." He shouted, and the solitary waiter, who was out in the street listening to the uproar, came reluctantly back to take the order.

Laura took a mouthful from the glass that was put in front of her, and spluttered. It was neat schnapps. It tasted like incandescent hair oil.

"Finish it," said Helmut. "You won't like it, but it will do you good."

"I'm all right now."

"What were you crashing about in the crowd for? They were beginning to get angry about it."

"It was the man," said Laura.

"Which man?"

"He was quite young. He had fair hair, and a— rather pretty face. You know—sort of weak, but pretty. He was coming out of the theater."

"And you suddenly felt an overmastering desire to chase this—what would you say?—an actor or perhaps a pop singer."

"It's not a joke."

"It would have been no joke for him if you had caught him, I can see."

Laura said angrily, "Will you stop making fun of me? The man was a murderer."

Helmut stared at her.

"I told you. He was slipping out of the theater by a side door. And I recognized him."

"You recognized him?"

"You remember my telling you, at dinner last

night, about that gang of bullies that was beating up an Italian. Well, he was the leader of them."

Helmut signaled to the waiter and ordered more schnapps.

"I'd rather have coffee," said Laura.

"*And* coffee. Now see if I can set this straight. Because you recognized this man as someone you had seen assaulting an Italian the night before, you came to the conclusion that he had had a hand in shooting the Bishop."

"I saw him do it."

"You—?"

"No, that's not quite right. I saw a gun being pointed at the Bishop through a gap in one of the circular windows in the turret beside the porch."

"Then what—a flash—smoke."

What *had* she seen? She shut her eyes. Had the gun barrel jumped just a little, as the shots rang out? When she opened her eyes again Helmut was looking at her, his head cocked, the eighth of a smile on his lips.

"You don't believe it, do you?" she said. "You don't believe a single word of it."

"The idea in my part of the crowd," said Helmut, "was that the shooting was done by an Italian. I didn't see him myself, but lots of people seem to have seen him. A big man, with black hair. He was shouting and waving while the Bishop was speaking; then he pulled out a gun and shot him."

"There *was* a man."

"You saw him, then?"

"He was with a group of people under a lamppost opposite where I was sitting. But he didn't do the shooting. That was done from the theater."

"By your blond friend?"

"Well—of course, I don't know it was him. But if he wasn't mixed up in it, why was he sneaking out of the theater by the back way?"

"Maybe he works there," said Helmut. "He sounds a bit theatrical. Suppose he was watching the parade from one of the theater windows."

"Why did he run away when he saw me?"

"*That*," said Helmut, "I agree is *quite* inexplicable. Hello. What's all this?"

There was a crescendo of noise in the street outside, and three open lorries rocketed past. Each of them was full of uniformed, steel-helmeted men.

"Reservists," said Helmut. "Colonel Julius is doing his stuff."

"Colonel Julius?"

"Julius Schatzmann, otherwise the Gray Bear, our respected Sicherheits direktor, or chief of security. It was Julius himself who got onto the microphone after the shooting. Didn't you hear him?"

"I heard someone bellowing. I didn't understand it."

The man who had served them with drinks came up and said something to Helmut.

"He's turning us out."

"Why?"

"He's from Italy himself. He thinks there's going to be trouble."

The man, stocky and black-haired, was clearly on edge for them to go. A boy—his son, she guessed—was already swinging a heavy shutter across one of the windows.

"It mightn't be a bad idea," said Helmut. He seemed in no hurry to move, however, but was lying back in his chair, feeling in his pocket for money. "I should think that the consulate would be the safest place for you."

"What sort of trouble?" said Laura. "What do you mean?"

Outside, from the direction of the square, came a sharp rattling. It was as if someone had drawn a walking stick along a section of iron railing. The sound ceased as abruptly as it had started.

"A machine gun," said Helmut. "I wonder who's shooting whom?" He handed the man some money, and they walked to the door and looked cautiously out.

The street was empty.

"Stay where you are for a moment," said Helmut. "I've got my car down the next turning."

Most of the shops in the little street were shut, she noticed, the doors barred and the windows shuttered. At first-floor level faces peered from curtained windows.

Then the car slid up.

"Jump in," said Helmut, "and don't look so worried. Everything's under control now, I imagine."

"I'm quite all right," said Laura.

The noise from the square had died down.

There were occasional shouts, but they seemed to be the shouts of people in authority. Over all, the loudspeaker boomed steadily. Then the voice stopped speaking, there was a crackling, and music blared out.

In the Maria-Theresien-Strasse they ran into a roadblock. Two troop carriers were across the street. Helmut spoke to the young, good-looking sergeant of gendarmerie, and they were allowed to pass.

"The sergeant seemed to know you," said Laura.

"He ought to," said Helmut. "He was on my ski team last year."

"Why are they blocking the roads?"

"That's Julius. It's his idea of security. If anything happens, you put a cordon round, quick. You can work out the answers later. The first thing is to keep everyone where they are."

"Was he expecting trouble?"

Helmut looked at her sideways out of his brown eyes, and said, "He was brought up in a hard school. Here we are. I expect your brother will be back soon."

He parked the car, walked with her into the hallway of the flats, and pressed the button for the lift.

"Would you like me to come up with you?"

"I shall be all right," she said. "Frau Rosa will be there."

"If you do want me for anything, please telephone me. I shall be only too pleased. Here. I will give you my card. It has my telephone number on it."

"You've been very kind," she said.

"There was one other thing I wanted to say. You may find this strange. I think it would be wiser to forget all that you may have seen, or may not have seen, in the square. Eyes play strange tricks. I have seen that myself, on the mountains. Once I very clearly saw my friend, above me, reach down and cut the rope between us. I saw the knife, I saw the strands in the rope part, one by one. Then I blinked my eyes—and none of it had happened. It was an optical illusion, brought on by strain and sleeplessness. Auf wiedersehen."

He gave an absurd little click with his heels, swung about, and was gone.

Laura shut the lift door, and pressed the button which would take her up to her brother's flat on the top floor. "But I wasn't suffering from strain." She said it aloud as if Helmut were in the lift with her. "Or sleeplessness. And I've got particularly good eyesight," she added, as she fitted the key into the lock. "Frau Rosa!"

There was no answer. Frau Rosa was evidently out, shopping or watching the parade. Laura went to look in the kitchen, and shouted once more to make sure. But the flat was empty.

In the drawing room there was a copy of the thin-paper edition of the *Times* that Charles got every day, twenty-four hours after publication. It carried on the editorial page an account of troubles in the South Tyrol headlined "When Neighbours

Fall Out." She read a few sentences of it, but the reasonable, cultivated phrases made no sense to her. She was seeing a fierce old man, with a white face and a nose like an eagle's beak, falling forward onto his knees, as if in prayer, and then folding forward onto his face. She was watching a red hat cartwheeling down the steps.

Bump, bump, bump. It was her own heart beating. She felt cold.

One of the double windows was open, and when she went across to shut it she noticed that the blue sky of the morning had gone. It was as if an artist, tiring of a summer scene, had dipped his brush in gray and blocked out the sky with a few quick strokes.

The telephone rang. Laura let it ring. She did not feel up to shaping German sentences. After a bit it got discouraged and stopped.

The shutting of the window had made the room very quiet. She picked up the paper again. "It is to be hoped," said the foreign correspondent of the *Times*, "that counsels of moderation will prevail, and that we shall not see, in these peaceful upland valleys, so loved of tourists, the incongruous incidents of terrorism and repressions."

Did journalists really hope that counsels of moderation would prevail? Or was it something they said while they sat by and hoped for exactly the opposite? She was pretty certain that counsels of moderation were the last thing Joe Keller wanted.

The thought of Joe was still in her mind when a

key clicked in the lock and, as she jumped to her feet, Charles came in, followed by a stout little man whom she remembered seeing seated next to him at the parade.

"My colleague, Dr. Pisoni, Italian Consul General," said Charles.

Dr. Pisoni bowed from the area which, in a differently constructed man, would have been his waist. He looked badly worried.

"Am I glad to see you!" said Laura to Charles. "Did you have any trouble getting back?"

"No trouble at all. And I hope it stays that way. Schatzmann seems to have everything under control."

"What happened?"

"The crowd tried to lynch Boschetto. The Colonel had half a dozen truckloads of gendarmerie in reserve, and he whistled them up. They got Boschetto away, but they had to shoot to do it."

"Who is Boschetto?"

Dr. Pisoni took this question. "He is an Italian from Bolzano. I understand that he has just been released, after a three-year prison sentence for assault and robbery."

"He must be mad," said Charles.

"No other explanation is possible," agreed Dr. Pisoni. It was a statement of diplomatic faith. "It was an unbelievable outrage. A Prince of the Church."

"And particularly unfortunate that it should have happened when—"

"Yes."

"When *what?*" asked Laura.

"Dr. Pisoni told me just before the parade. There was an unhappy incident in the South Tyrol last night—not far from Bolzano. A group of terrorists attacked an Italian police station. Two policemen were killed and three were injured. It would have been serious enough as an isolated incident. But now—"

Laura said, "Would Boschetto have known anything about it? If Dr. Pisoni had only learned about it through official circles?"

"News travels quickly in this part of the country."

"Especially bad news."

"All the same," said Laura, "a man like that. It's hard to believe that he would hear about it before it got into the papers."

"There was a personal involvement here," said Dr. Pisoni. "It is possible that Boschetto may have been given this news in advance of the general public. One of the policemen who was killed was his brother."

It was clear to Laura that this was news to Charles as well. For a moment the embryo diplomatic mask slipped and a look of honest excitement had taken its place. It made him look years younger.

Laura said, "That doesn't tie in very well with your first conclusion, does it? You said he was mad. If he had a brother killed by the Austrian terrorists, *and* got to know about it before it came out in the papers, *and* got hold of a gun, *and* got his own back by shooting an Austrian bishop—all inside twenty-four hours—he sounds to me a pretty smooth performer."

"Smooth?" said Dr. Pisoni anxiously.

"She means efficient," said Charles. And to Laura, "You seem to be taking all this very calmly. I suppose you realize that we're in the middle of the biggest diplomatic crisis in Austria since Dollfuss was assassinated."

Dr. Pisoni nodded energetically. "If it was thought that Boschetto had official support in this matter—that it was a reprisal—it could lead to almost any consequences."

"I thought he'd been in prison until yesterday," said Laura. "How *could he* possibly have any official support. He's a criminal."

"Governments have used criminals before now," said Charles.

"Well, I don't believe it. I think you were right the first time. He's just a madman. He'd probably had too much to drink. And he couldn't be stopped from waving his arms and shouting. His friends were trying to hold him down. I saw him. He was right opposite me."

"You *saw* him do the shooting?"

"Now look, Charles," said Laura, "let's get this quite straight. Boschetto did not shoot the Bishop."

"He was taken with a gun in his hand," said Dr. Pisoni. "Many people standing near him saw him pull it out, and saw him fire it, twice."

"I'm not denying that," said Laura. Now that the crisis had arrived she felt surprisingly calm.

74

"But the shots he fired went nowhere near the Bishop. He was struggling with the people standing around him. The shots probably went straight up into the air."

"It is more probable, I agree," said Dr. Pisoni, "but we have the fact. The Cardinal Bishop was shot. If not by Boschetto, then by whom?"

"He was shot twice, quite deliberately, from a turret window beside the portico of the theater. I saw the gun."

Dr. Pisoni looked at her. His round face had become suddenly shrewd. It was as if he was weighing her as a witness in a court of law.

"You saw the gun?"

"I saw more than the gun," said Laura. "When I was getting away from the square I saw the man who had used it. He was slipping out of the theater by a side door. And I not only saw him, but I recognized him. *And* I should be able to recognize him again."

6

A Chat with
the Gray Bear

"VIENNA FOR YOU," said the exchange.

"Lienz consulate here," said Charles. "Is that you, Piers?"

"Nice to hear your voice, Charles," said Piers Marrinder, First Secretary of the British Embassy at Vienna. "What can I do for you?"

"Is Uncle Horace there?"

"He's in his room."

"What's he doing?"

"Last time I was in there he was gnawing his nails."

"I meant, is he tied up with anyone?"

"No, he's quite alone. Would you like me to put you through?"

"That was the idea."

"When you've finished talking to him, ask the switchboard to put you back to me."

"All right, but why?"

"I met a girl at a British Council drink party last

night, called Penelope. She said she knew you at Oxford."

"I knew three girls called Penelope at Oxford."

"This one's got bronze-colored hair, and a tiny, tiny little mole in the middle of her shoulder blades."

"Oh, *that* one."

"Was she—did you find her forthcoming—you know what I mean?"

"I know exactly what you mean. And the answer's no."

"Oh. Well, I'd better put you through."

"Good morning, sir," said Charles. "I was ringing to find out if you'd read my yesterday's dispatch."

"Yes," said Sir Horace Lowry cautiously, "I read it."

"I didn't intend to discuss it—not on the telephone—"

"Naturally," said Sir Horace. They were both perfectly well aware that the line on which they were speaking was an open one and that everything they said was being recorded verbatim, and probably translated into three different languages.

"What I did wonder was whether the commercial aspects of it had struck you. I hardly had time in my preliminary report to stress them, but—"

"I hadn't thought about that, no. But now that you mention it, I think you're right. There are bound to be trade repercussions. I don't know a lot about that side myself. Would you like me to send our commercial adviser?"

"I think it might be an idea, sir. You've got a new man, haven't you?"

"Evelyn Fiennes. He came out last month. He used to be in Ankara."

"I should think he'd be just the sort of man we'd want," said Charles. "A good, practical man, I've always heard."

"Oh, yes. Extremely practical. I'd better give him his marching orders at once. Another twenty-four hours, and he won't be able to get to you by the direct route."

"It looks pretty threatening from here," said Charles.

"It's snowing on the Gross Glockner now. They can usually keep the road open for a bit. I'll tell Evelyn to pack straight away."

"Thank you, sir," said Charles. "I wonder if you could put me back to Piers for a moment."

"I heard all that," said Piers. "I gather you're pinching Evelyn. Don't keep him too long."

"You should have him back as soon as he's done his stuff."

"Watch out if he tries to get you into a game of liar dice. I owe him thirty-seven pounds already."

"That doesn't mean Evelyn's crooked. It just means you're a bad player. There was something I wanted to tell you. I believe I was wrong."

"Wrong about what?"

"About that girl. The one with the mole on her back *was* forthcoming."

*   *   *

78

"There's a man called Evelyn Fiennes coming out from Vienna," said Charles at lunchtime that day. "That's to say, if he doesn't get stuck on the Gross Glockner."

Laura looked out the window. Out of a leaden sky the snowflakes had begun to slip down, fat, lazy, and solid.

"Who's he?"

"He calls himself a commercial counselor."

"When you say he calls himself that, I suppose you mean he's something quite different."

"He's actually our cloak-and-dagger expert. I've never met him but I'm told he's very experienced."

"Secret Service, do you mean?"

"That sort of thing. I thought he might be a useful man to have around if anything starts. Anything involving us, I mean."

"What sort of thing?" It was very cozy in the flat, with its English sofa covers, and cushions, and shelves of books, and family photographs, and Charles's old pipes in a rack, and a water color on the wall of Penzance painted by their mad aunt Sylvia.

"I've no idea. At the moment it's a sort of private fight between the Austrians and the Italians. Dr. Pisoni's taking it very seriously. So is his government. The border of Sillian and the Brenner had been closed."

"Closed? How could they?"

"Not officially closed. But they've instituted a special visa, which you can't get at the frontier. So anyone who wants to get through has to go back to

Bolzano. It amounts to the same thing."

"I see," said Laura. She looked out again at the drifting snow. "If the frontier's shut at Sillian, and the Gross Glockner's blocked by snow, just how does anyone get to Lienz—or out of it, for that matter?"

"There's a lower road, to Villach and Klagenfurt. But if we get any real snow, that gets blocked too."

"Could you fly?"

"There isn't an airfield near Lienz that I'd care to land on. Not in this weather."

The telephone in the entrance hall rang, and Charles went out to answer it. Laura resumed her inspection of the street. The centers of the road were still black and shiny, but the snow was piling in the gutters and on the outer edges of the pavement.

Charles came back.

"Better get your hat and coat," he said. "We're wanted. That was Colonel Julius."

"He wants *us*?"

"Actually, it's you he asked for. But I think I'd better come along too, don't you?"

Laura said, "You needn't imagine I'm going alone."

"She is the younger sister of the British Vice-Consul, Hart. She spent three weeks in Rome before coming here."

"In *Rome!*"

"That is so, Colonel."

"Where before that?"

"She came straight from England. Or so she said. She was recuperating from an illness."

"That is the first time I have ever heard of Rome as a sanatorium," growled Colonel Schatzmann.

"I understand that the illness was not very serious. It was more a holiday than a convalescence."

"Hm. And what had her brother to say to his superiors in Vienna?"

Major Osler consulted his notes. "Ostensibly," he said, "the object of the telephone call was to ask for the assistance of the commercial adviser. That was clearly a blind."

"Yes."

"The real message was in code. The significant words were 'Penelope' and 'mole.' There was also a reference to the game of dice."

"And the meaning of it?"

"Our cipher department is working on it now."

"Good." The buzzer on the Colonel's desk sounded, and he picked up the receiver and listened to the message. Then he said to Osler, "It is Miss Hart. Her brother is with her. I do not think we can refuse to allow him to be present."

"It might be more proper."

The Colonel rose to his feet. He really did look remarkably like a bear balancing on its hind legs. He scratched the back of his thick neck and said, "I was not thinking of propriety. I was thinking of tactics. If her brother is with her, I think I will have Inspector Moll here—get him, will you?—and Dr. Kippinger."

It looked like a selection board, thought Laura, when she was shown into the room. The huge man in the middle must be Colonel Schatzmann. The stolid, flat-faced person on his right was a policeman in any language. The third man looked like a scientist. He had white hair, a trim mouth, and inverted semicircular glasses which had slipped down the knife-edge of his nose.

"It was kind of you to come," said the Colonel. Like many Austrian officials, he spoke very passable English. "I am afraid that Inspector Moll—" the man, hearing his name, inclined his head briefly—"does not speak English, and I shall have to interpret for him. Your brother will see that I do this fairly."

"We would not for a moment imagine that you would do anything else," said Charles.

"I am a policeman. You are a diplomat. We are both used to being misinterpreted. Now, Miss Hart. You were a witness of the shocking affair this morning. I understand that you have important evidence to offer."

Laura took her courage into her hands.

"When you say you *understand* that, Colonel, do you mean that you have had some report about me?"

"Yes, I have had a report."

"Am I allowed to ask from whom?"

"You are allowed to ask." The Colonel's face broke into an alarming smile. "And I will tell you. It was your brother's Italian colleague, Dr. Pisoni."

Charles said, "It was quite improper of him to

repeat a private conversation. If I had wished him to make a statement to you, we should have done it through the ordinary channels."

"Most improper," agreed the Colonel. "But I doubt if Dr. Pisoni was troubling about the niceties of diplomatic procedure. He was concerned with the fate of the assassin. Boschetto is an Italian-speaking citizen of the South Tyrol, and as such it is Dr. Pisoni's duty to assist him—if he can."

"All the same—"

"But we are allowing ourselves to be diverted." He turned back to Laura. "Have you any objection to repeating, officially, in front of us, what you have already said, unofficially, to Dr. Pisoni?"

She took a quick look at Charles, but there was no help there. The decision was hers.

"No," she said, "I have no objection."

"Very well, then—"

"Just before the shots were fired, I happened to be looking at the theater. There are three circular windows in the left-hand turret—the left hand as you look at it, that is."

"Yes?" said the Colonel.

The flat-faced policeman was writing steadily.

"As I looked at it, it was opened a fraction, and I saw the barrel of a gun come through."

"What color is the paint on the window?"

"What—I'm not sure. Yellow, I think. Why?"

"You were sitting—what?—thirty yards away from a window—the paint is dark green, in fact—it opened a fraction—and you saw the barrel of a gun coming through. Saw it, and were able, in a flash, to identify it. Really, Miss Hart. *How* did you identify it?"

"The light was reflected from it."

"And if the light is reflected from an object—" the Colonel absentmindedly picked up a silver pencil from his desk as he spoke—"it follows that it *must* be a gun barrel?"

"I have quite exceptional eyesight."

"Most exceptional," agreed the Colonel. "Did you see the bullets leaving the gun and flying toward the Bishop?"

"Of course not."

"I think," said Charles, "that you would be well advised to take my sister's story seriously. Whether what she says is correct or not, she certainly saw something. It is, to put it at its lowest, an odd coincidence that it should have happened when it did. And I think it should be investigated."

"If I did not take it seriously," said the Colonel, "I should not have asked you to come here. And the story has been investigated, to the best of our ability. I shall hope to be able to convince your sister that what she saw was an optical illusion— an effect of light and shade—not a reality at all." He turned to his right-hand companion. "Inspector Moll, would you be good enough to tell Miss Hart the result of your investigations so far?"

Inspector Moll spoke quietly. After three or four sentences the Colonel held his hand up.

"Allow Mr. Hart to translate," he said.

"The inspector says that immediately after the shooting he ran across, himself, to the center of disturbance, under the lamppost. Three men were hanging onto a fourth—Boschetto—and Boschetto had, actually in his hand—an automatic pistol, which the others were preventing him from firing. He says that he took the pistol from him and, after Boschetto had been arrested, handed the pistol straight over to the head of the police laboratory for testing."

"Proceed, Inspector," said the Colonel.

"After that," said Charles, "he says he had a thorough search of the scene made and one bullet was found embedded in the woodwork of the pillar, about eight feet up from the base point of the pillar. The inspector says he—I didn't quite get that bit."

Inspector Moll spoke at length, demonstrating with his hands.

"Yes, I see. He cut out a small, cubic section of the woodwork of the pillar, containing the bullet, and handed it over to Dr. Kippinger here. The doctor is in charge of the forensic science department."

Dr. Kippinger said, in rusty, unaccented English, "I have the bullets." He extracted from a briefcase a large envelope and shook from it two smaller, transparent containers.

"This I designate 'A.' It is the bullet that lodged near the spine of the Bishop. It was taken from the body by our pathologist, Dr. Krauss, and you will see that he has identified it by his initials on the envelope. This I designate 'B.' It is the bullet handed to me by Inspector Moll."

"Had he taken it out of the wood?" asked Charles.

"No. It was still embedded in the wood, which it had penetrated in an upward direction."

"How do you know that?"

"I do not follow."

"If the inspector gave you a small square of wood with a bullet in it, how do you know what angle the bullet came from? Unless you, yourself, went back to the pillar and fitted the piece of wood into it, to see which way up it went."

The doctor looked surprised, and spoke to Inspector Moll, who answered him in rapid German.

The Colonel said with a smile, "Your point was well made, Mr. Hart. But it appears that the inspector, being a careful police officer, when he cut the piece of wood from the pillar, marked the top."

"All right," said Charles. "I just wanted to know."

"I then," said the doctor, "fired a bullet from the gun which had been removed from the prisoner Boschetto. The bullet was fired into a closed box, and recovered. I placed it with exhibit A, in a comparison microscope, and I have here photographs—they are six times enlarged—"

He laid on the table a mounted photograph. Laura and Charles peered down at it. It looked like a stereoscopic slide, except that the two halves of the photograph were nearly, not precisely, identical.

"If you will look closely you can see the marked

similarities. The striations in the soft driving band —you observe how their sequence is repeated in both cases." He produced another photograph. "This is the base of the cartridge that I fired, compared with the base of a cartridge found by the police in the gutter, under the lamppost."

Laura looked again. Even to her eye, this time, the similarity was apparent.

"You observe how the firing pin has struck noticeably to the left of the center point, and with a slight inclination toward the circumference."

"You're telling us," said Charles, "that the two bullets—one of which lodged in the body of the Bishop and one of which struck him in the shoulder and ended up in the pillar behind him— that they were both, definitely, fired from the gun taken from Boschetto."

"That is the inescapable deduction," said the doctor.

"You must, I think, see the force of this," said the Colonel to Laura.

"I suppose so."

"*If* the assassin was, indeed, a man who secreted himself in the theater and fired from the window, as you have described, how did he transfer his gun into the possession of a man standing twenty yards away, in full view, in the middle of the square?"

"Couldn't two different guns make the same sort of mark?"

The Colonel turned to Dr. Kippinger, who shook his head so emphatically that his glasses nearly fell off.

"That is quite impossible," he said. "Rifling marks are as distinct as fingerprints. And as reliable. I have never examined bullets from different guns which have appeared even superficially alike. A modern comparison microscope measures similarities—and dissimilarities—to a thousandth of a millimeter."

"Reflect also," said the Colonel, "that the first bullet lodged in the pillar eight feet above ground level. The window is—what? I have not measured it exactly, but should we say ten feet up? For the bullet to have struck the Bishop in the shoulder he must have been at least nine feet high."

"Unless it was deflected," said Laura.

"Possible. But unlikely, don't you think?"

"Well—" said Charles.

Laura detected the weakening in his voice. She said, "Has anyone looked at the window?"

There was a very slight pause. Then the Colonel said, "I am not sure what you mean, Miss Hart."

"I suppose it opens into some sort of room or staircase inside the turret. Has anyone been up there to see if the window has been tampered with?"

The Colonel said something to Inspector Moll, who seemed, like his superior officer, to be taken off balance by the question. It was momentary only.

"You have caught us out, Miss Hart," said the Colonel. "As you perceive, we attached so little weight to your story that we did not take the very elementary step you have suggested. It can easily be remedied. Come along."

A police car took the four of them to the theater. "I have had the caretaker telephoned. He will let us in by the stage door. The front of the theater is still cordoned."

The caretaker, a sad-faced little man, met them at the stage door. He bowed to the Colonel and conducted them along passages which twisted and turned back on themselves like the larger intestine of a whale; down breakneck stairs; through a fireproof door, and out through the sheeted auditorium, into the foyer.

Here he unlocked a small door beside the box office.

"This leads, you understand, Herr Oberst, only to the electricians' gallery."

"Understood," said the Colonel. "Have you any lights?"

"A moment."

The caretaker went into the box office, fumbled in the half-darkness, and found the right switch. A pale bulb showed them the interior of the turret, with the stairs leading upward.

The air was stale, and there was a very faint smell of dry rot.

At the first landing the Colonel halted. In front of him was a door. He tried it, and found it locked.

"What is in here?"

"It is a small room, Herr Oberst. The electricians use it for their stuff."

"Open it, please."

After some searching the caretaker found the key that fitted the lock, and pushed open the door. It was, as he had said, a very small room, opening into an embrasure in the turret.

"Would this be the window?"

"I think it must be," said Laura. She stepped forward, and the Colonel said, "I should advise care."

It was a timely warning. The floor, the window ledge, and the window itself were thick with dust.

The caretaker said apologetically, "Had I known you wished to come here, I would have had the room cleaned. It is a long time since it has been used."

7

Evelyn Fiennes

As Charles drove into the forecourt of the municipal buildings his headlights, probing the swirling snow, picked out some of the significant changes that had been made in the past twenty-four hours. Barbed wire, in concertina rolls, now confined approaching traffic to one double lane. Across the approach stretched a counterweighted steel girder, operated from a sandbagged, loop-holed barrier. Two troop carriers had been backed behind the barrier, and from their dark interiors he caught a metallic flash as a machine gun swung on its tripod mounting.

Charles produced his diplomatic pass, the sentry raised the pole, and he drove into the inner courtyard.

When he got out he found the sergeant of the guard standing beside him.

"Kindly not to lock your car."

"Why on earth not?"

"Orders."

Charles stared at him. He recognized the sergeant, an old regular soldier.

"What's it all about?" he said.

"We had trouble here earlier in the day. All cars have to be left open, so that they can, if necessary, be searched."

"If anyone searches my car there's going to be twenty different sorts of trouble."

"I do not imagine that it will be necessary in your case, Herr Konsul. Come with me, please."

The building seemed full of soldiers. Some of them were regulars, but most of them were wearing the armbands of the auxiliary forces.

When Charles was shown into his office, Hofrat Humbold indicated a chair and came to the point without further preliminary.

"I gather," he said, "that you are now convinced that the story being put about by your sister has no foundation in fact."

Charles blinked. The friendly dinner guest had, indeed, disappeared. It was the head of state talking, and talking to a very junior vice-consul.

"I'm not sure that I've reached any conclusion on the point yet."

"You have been shown the evidence."

"I have been shown some evidence."

"What other conclusion can there be than that his Eminence was assassinated by the Italian Boschetto?"

"I should like to correct the record in one particular," said Charles. "My sister's story—as you call it—is not being put about by her, or by anyone. She talked, in confidence, to me and to my Italian colleague. For reasons best known to himself, Dr. Pisoni passed the information on to Colonel Schatzmann. If anyone has publicized her story, it would appear to be your officials."

"She has repeated it to no one else?"

"So far as I am aware, no."

"Then how do you account for the fact that one of my personal aides learned of this fiction from Herr Helmut Angel?"

"I imagine he heard it from Colonel Schatzmann or Dr. Pisoni."

"Within thirty minutes of the shooting."

Charles hoped that he did not look as shaken as he felt. He decided to counterattack.

"Herr Hofrat," he said, "if you, and your police, are perfectly convinced that my sister's story is incorrect, why do you attach any importance to it at all?"

"Do you really wish to know, or is the question a rhetorical one?"

"I certainly wish to know."

Dr. Humbold rose to his feet, walked across to the long window that overlooked the inner courtyard, and stood for a full minute in the shadows, looking out at the falling snow. Charles waited. Experience had inured him to the Hofrat's theatrical devices. Nevertheless, when he finally turned and came back into the light, Charles was startled by the expression on his face.

(He said afterward to Laura, "If you were walking with a man you didn't know very well along the edge of a cliff, and looked up suddenly, and saw that he had just made up his mind to push you over—you'd have some sort of idea of the way he looked.")

"This morning," said Humbold, "just after midday, a private car drove into the inner courtyard. The driver had a pass, and gave the name of one of our medical officers, of the Health Department. The sentry let him in. He entered the building and, as we found out later, walked straight out of it on the other side, and disappeared. By chance the sentry mentioned the matter to the guard commander, who happened to know that the medical officer in question was in Vienna. He examined the car, and found the back and the luggage compartment packed with explosives, attached to a firing and timing device in the front seat. The sergeant disconnected the firing apparatus and our experts took over the car. It was parked"—Humbold indicated the window—"immediately outside there. It contained sufficient explosives to bring down this part of the building."

"Allow me to congratulate you," said Charles, "both personally and on behalf of Her Majesty's government, on your fortunate escape."

"Thank you," said Humbold. "I gave you this information in answer to your question. You will perhaps see its relevance now."

"You mean that you are expecting further trouble."

"I mean that we are in a very grave state of

emergency. All the graver, that there has been no communication with Vienna since nightfall."

"Snow?"

"It might be snow, but that seems unlikely. The cable through the mountains goes underground. The snow would not affect it."

"Sabotage?"

"I think it very probable. At all events, I am taking no chances. While we are isolated from the capital, I have a responsibility to the state."

"Yes," said Charles. He wondered what was coming.

"A decree has been drafted, declaring a state of emergency in the district. I am signing it tonight. Cases of sabotage and incitement to disorder will be punishable before a military tribunal. I am restoring the death penalty—for crimes against the state."

"Surely," said Charles, "such very stringent measures are not called for—yet. As soon as communications are restored—"

"Last winter we were cut off from the rest of the country for eight weeks. It was not serious, because we had easy access through the South Tyrol and the Brenner. That is not now the case."

"No."

"Are you questioning my measures?"

"The responsibility for public order rests entirely on the shoulders of the Herr Hofrat," said Charles.

"I do not welcome it," said Humbold. "Neither do I shirk it." He added, "I am telling you this so that you will understand why your sister has to leave Lienz at once."

"How?"

"She has a British passport. She may be delayed at the Italian frontier, but I hardly think she will be stopped."

"Yes," said Charles. "But—" He broke off.

"You were about to add, 'but why?'" said Humbold. "Then you perceived that the question was a stupid one, and you refrained from asking it. I am glad that you are beginning to appreciate the realities of the situation. Would you kindly return now and make arrangements for your sister? The express train for Rome leaves at ten minutes to midnight."

Laura had made her own way back to the flat from the theater. She had walked slowly. She wanted time to think.

The condition of the room in the theater—the thick dust on the floor, the cobwebs on the windows, the general air of a room which has stood undisturbed for months or years—had been convincing. It had been extremely convincing. Had it not been almost too convincing?

When had the theater last been used? A week—perhaps a fortnight—earlier. The posters were still up. Then should the room be quite as dusty as that? It had electricians' stuff in it. It might not be used a lot, but it would be used occasionally. Yet the depth of dust on the floor suggested a room which hadn't been opened for a century. It looked as if someone had taken a giant insufflator—something like a vacuum cleaner in reverse—and blown dust over everything, spreading it thick and even, like icing on a cake.

If that was so, there was a considerable organization at work: an organization able to put a man into that room with a gun which—she had no idea how—but which, somehow, matched the bullets in Boschetto's gun, and get him away afterward, and clear away all signs of his presence under a coating of dust, and, probably, square the janitor.

Charles had given her a key to the flat and she let herself in. The noise of the front door brought Frau Rosa from the kitchen. She said, in her slow, careful German, "There is a gentleman in the front room."

"Who is he, Frau Rosa?"

"A diplomatic gentleman. His name I do not know."

Laura got rid of her hat and coat, executed some quick repairs to her face, and made her way along to the sitting room. She hoped that the representative of the Diplomatic Corps would not stay too long or prove too talkative.

Sprawled on the sofa, reading the *Times*, was a man in his early forties. He had the sort of stubborn, black beard that needs to be shaved twice a day; dark eyebrows which ran toward each other and then, at the last moment, turned upward, like two men on a pavement trying to avoid each other,

97

and stepping the same way; a thick nose, and a rounded chin.

Despite the dark hair he was quite clearly English. His manners alone guaranteed that.

He made a minimal gesture of one starting to get to his feet, found the effort too much for him, and said, "Good evening. My name is Fiennes. Evelyn Fiennes. You must be the problem child."

"I beg your pardon?"

"It is Miss Hart, isn't it?"

"It is."

"And it was you who put out the story about a hidden assassin in the theater?"

Laura said, "I didn't put out anything. I told my brother what I had seen. And I'm not at all sure I ought to discuss it with you."

"Oh, *I'm* all right. I'm on your side. You can talk to me."

"How do I know that?"

"You don't, really, that's true. I might be one of Colonel Julius' undercover boys, trying to lure you on to further indiscretions. Or I might be a reporter from the Lienz *Herald*, out for a scoop."

"If you had been," said Laura, "I don't imagine you'd have helped yourself to quite so much of my brother's whisky."

"I needed it," said Fiennes. "I have come fast and far. Like young Lochinvar, who, you will remember, came out of the west. In all the wide border his steed was the best. I came from Vienna in a prewar Austin, with chains on the wheels, and I don't mind betting that not many people got over the Gross Glockner after me."

"Wonderful," said Laura. "What was all the hurry about?"

"You."

"Why should Vienna be worried about me?"

"To be honest, I don't really know. Like the Light Brigade, I never question my orders, however apparently fatuous."

"I see."

"I was once sent all the way from Athens to meet a certain lady at the Gare du Nord, and escort her across Paris to the Gare de Lyons. It transpired that my chiefs thought I was in Paris at the time. And sent me a top-secret signal, which was, of course, forwarded to me in Ankara, and reforwarded to me in Athens. I caught the Qantas jet to Rome and reached the Gare du Nord with five minutes to spare. It was a waste of effort. The lady had died at Calais."

"What of?" asked Laura politely.

"Old age."

"I see. What an exciting life you must lead. Now. I wonder if you could answer my question. Why did you have to come all this way, in such a hurry?"

"You really want to know? Then I suggest you pour yourself a drink—I'd do it for you, but I expect you know exactly how you like it. And while you're at it a small one for me. Not *quite* as small as that. Thank you. The truth is, you're in rather a delicate situation."

"I'm afraid I can't see it."

"Well, I expect you haven't really tried yet."

Laura gave him a freezing look, but the effort was wasted. He was engrossed in extracting ice cubes for his own whisky.

"Humbold," said Fiennes, having arranged his drink to his satisfaction, "is three quarters of a great man. He's got patience, drive, and imagination. He's a good organizer. And he's ruthless. The Austrian government think they sent him out here to get rid of him. I shouldn't be at all surprised if Humbold didn't arrange the whole thing. Lienz is an ideal base for an unscrupulous man. For months at a time it's very difficult to get at—particularly if the Italian border's shut. Accessibility. That's one of the drawbacks of your up-and-coming dictator. Before he's really got under way with his dictating, some interfering person from higher up comes along and calls time."

"What could he *do*?"

"Ultimately, you mean. I don't think anyone knows that for sure. If he gets the temperature high enough, I suppose he could move in and liberate the South Tyrol—join it to Lienz—declare an independent state."

"He couldn't do that."

"Who'd stop him?"

"Italy—Austria—No, Italy."

"Make your mind up. If Italy moved against him they'd have Austria to cope with. And not only Austria. Germany as well. There are a lot of Nazis in the Tiroler Boden Bund."

"But—an independent state—it'd be much too small."

"No smaller than Albania. Bigger than Luxembourg or Liechtenstein."

"I don't believe the UN would allow it."

"You mustn't make me laugh," said Fiennes. "I've got a weak heart. Why should the Afro-Asian bloc countries stop the Tyrolese doing what they're doing themselves? Self-determination! Down with the stinking colonialists from Vienna! The UN wouldn't stop them. Even if they wanted to, they couldn't. It'd be against Rule One in the United Nations Charter. Never interfere with a fait accompli."

"Even if he wanted to do it, how could he possibly?"

"Ah! Now you're asking. I don't know the answer to that. But it's wonderful what you can do when you get people excited enough."

"He hasn't got an army."

"He's got what he calls a Security Force. It's a mixture of police and reservists. And they've got tanks and artillery. They could take over the South Tyrol like picking an apple. They'd only have a handful of Italian police to deal with. And once they're in, with three quarters of the population backing them, I don't see who's going to get them out again. Do you?"

Laura said nothing. She was seeing the face of the frightened little Italian in the grip of the three bullies. It wasn't going to be much fun for the Italian minority in the Tyrol if Humbold really was planning a private Anschluss.

"Of course, that's all surmise," said Fiennes. "But he's up to something. Something which depends on getting everybody as worked up as possible. And there's nothing more calculated to get Austrians worked up than shooting a cardinal bishop."

"He wasn't—he didn't seem to be—a very saintly man."

"He had rather a rough time in the war. I believe he was one of the few men who was tortured by the Germans *and* the Russians."

Laura saw the red hat rolling down the steps. She felt sick. Sick of intrigue; sick of violence; sick of blood.

Fiennes said, "We've got two possibilities here. Either the thing was unpremeditated, and Humbold is grabbing his chance with both hands. Or else he organized the whole thing. The chap who's supposed to have done the shooting—Albin Boschetto—he was only two days out of jail. It wouldn't have been impossible—either to indoctrinate him or to strike a bargain with him."

"He *didn't* kill the Bishop," said Laura.

"I was coming to that," said Fiennes. "You could easily be right. If I'd organized a drunken jailbird to shoot at someone and it was pretty essential for him to hit him, I don't think I should take his marksmanship for granted. After all, it'd be a thousand pities if he missed. So I think I might have a second gun posted in the wings, just to make sure."

"Then you believe me?"

"I think so, yes."

"Thank heavens, someone does."

"But it doesn't solve your problem, which is that no one else in Lienz is going to believe you. Every time you open your mouth you're going to be branded as a dangerous agent of counterrevolution."

"Don't worry," said Laura. She had made her mind up five minutes before. "I'm not going to open my mouth. It's nothing to do with me."

Fiennes looked at her curiously.

"You know," he said, "what you need is a good night's rest. . . . That sounds like Charles."

Charles came in, said, "Hullo, Evelyn, so you got here all right. I expect you've introduced yourselves."

"We have," said Laura.

"I ought to have warned you about Evelyn. He's got no manners. And he drinks too much."

"I've got other vices as well," said Evelyn. "But we've only known each other for a quarter of an hour."

"It's going to be a case of hail and farewell," said Charles. "She's catching the midnight train for Rome."

"But—" said Laura.

"Can he do that?" said Fiennes. "What about diplomatic privilege?"

"I wouldn't know," said Charles. "But I'm not arguing about it. It's an order from the boss. And I think, on this occasion, we're going to do what we're told."

They both looked at Laura.

"Is there really going to be trouble?" she said.

"I don't know," said Charles. "But I'm quite sure of this: that whatever does happen, you'll only aggravate it if you're here."

"All right," she said. "I'll get packed."

"Have you got somewhere you can stay in Rome?"

"I'll be all right."

As she went out, Fiennes said, "Talking about trouble, it looks as if something's starting right now."

From the window they could see, beyond the black bulk of the railway station, red and orange flames and, lit by the flames, a billow of smoke.

"Open the window," said Fiennes.

The two men stood at the open window and listened. The swelling sound of the mob came clearly to them through the frosty night air. Then a single shot. Then a burst of firing.

"It sounds to me," said Fiennes, "as if things were hotting up a bit. I'd better go and have a look."

"Don't get involved in anything."

"Don't worry. There are few people who can run faster than I can."

Charles sighed, and poured himself a drink.

He and Laura were sitting down to a silent dinner when Fiennes returned.

"Quite a party," he said. "The crowd started by

looting some Italian shops and then set fire to the Italian church. The police seem to have had orders not to interfere—or not to interfere too soon— anywhere. They fired a few shots in the air to show their zeal. A fire engine arrived, and got turned over. The only person who made any real attempt to keep the peace was Radler."

"The Socialist?"

"I don't know about his politics. But he's got a voice like a foghorn. And plenty of guts. He got up on the fire engine and fairly let them have it."

"What did he say?"

"He told them not to be bloody fools. And to go home before someone really got hurt. Good, sound stuff. The fire was nearly out by then, and it had started to snow. I don't think there'll be any more trouble tonight."

"I hope not," said Charles. "We've got to get Laura to the station."

There was no trouble of any sort. The snow had stopped. They drove in silence through the empty streets, tires squeaking occasionally in the thick drifts, which were beginning to pack down as the temperature fell.

In the station waiting room a small crowd was standing in front of a bulletin board. Charles went across, looked at it, spoke to one of the station officials, and came back.

"Home to bed," he said. "There are no trains into or out of Lienz."

"It must have been snowing pretty hard," said Evelyn, "to block the line to Italy."

They were in the car and driving back to the flat before Charles answered this. He said, "It isn't snow that is stopping the trains. A three-span culvert has been dynamited. They reckon it'll take at least a week to repair."

8

"Dear Department—"

"DEAR DEPARTMENT," CHARLES TYPED, using one finger of each hand and paying careful attention to spacing and alignment, "the situation here has deteriorated since my last telephone communication on Thursday. It is not known yet whether the destruction of the culvert at Garvas was the work of Italian saboteurs from the Trentino, but it is generally attributed to them. This, coupled with the snow which has fallen"—Charles looked out the window of the consular office—"and is still falling, has isolated Lienz almost completely from the outside world."

He broke off once more. How was he to record, in the traditional language of the Foreign Service, pruned of all unnecessary adverbs and adjectives, an impression of impending disaster?

"This morning we were informed that Herr Radler, the leader of the Socialist opposition in the Landtag, and his deputy, Herr Hammerle, have both been placed under protective custody. Their offense, apparently, was haranguing the crowd that was burning the Italian church. Further reserve forces have been called up, and camps are being formed near the Italian frontier, ostensibly for road clearance. There is a curfew in the town of Lienz, but movement is not as yet restricted by day. A military tribunal is being set up to try Boschetto. I will add to this despatch from time to time, and will send it by the first available messenger. Yours ever, Consulate."

There were other points he considered mentioning: the curious difficulty he was experiencing in contacting his diplomatic colleagues, more particularly Dr. Pisoni. The fact that all telephone calls from his flat were now quite openly intercepted and listened to. The presence, on the other side of the road, of three gentlemen who took it in turns to watch the door of the house in which his flat stood.

Frau Rosa had pointed them out to Laura, with undisguised contempt. "If I wish that they should be allowed to follow me," she said, "then I allow them. If I do not wish it, I should not allow."

"How would you do that?" Laura asked.

"I have friends in this building. There would be no difficulty. On the ground floor, for instance, is the consulting room of Dr. Grill. He is Zahnarzt —Dentisten." Frau Rosa made the gesture of extracting a tooth. "From his kitchen you can go into the kitchen of the restaurant. There is a door in the wall."

"I don't expect they'd follow you anyway," said Laura, "even if you went out of the front door. It's me they're after."

Frau Rosa snorted. It was clear that she did not dislike the idea of being followed by police agents.

The telephone rang.

"For you," said Frau Rosa.

It was Helmut.

"Miss Hart. Nice to hear your voice. They haven't deported you yet?"

"They couldn't. No trains."

"Of course not. I had forgotten. It's an ill wind, as they say. I shall be able to implement my promise to you, and show you some of the night life of Lienz."

"I'm not sure if I'm allowed out," said Laura.

"Allowed?"

"There's a man watching the flat."

"He won't stop you. His orders will be to follow you. He can sit at the next table and watch us eat. By the way, you are aware that our conversation is being listened to?"

"No?"

"Certainly. Everything we say is being written down. We must be careful not to speak too fast. Dictation speed."

"Are you sure?"

"The gentleman now listening has asthma. If you listen carefully you can hear him."

In the silence that followed it did seem to Laura that she detected a faint, and embarrassed, clearing of the throat.

"I shall have to speak rather in riddles, then," said Helmut. "You remember the lady I was talking about when we had dinner together. The one who had a lighted cigarette end dropped down her back at an Olympic Reception."

"Her Christian name?"

"Her forename, yes. Let us meet there at eight o'clock this evening."

"I'll see if I can," said Laura.

Charles had pointed out the watchers to her but hadn't actually said that she was to stay indoors. It wasn't her fault if the way to the frontier was blocked. She wasn't breaking any law. She had been told to leave the country, and she would do so as soon as the way was clear. Meanwhile she saw no reason why she should mope about indoors, reading back numbers of the *Times*.

The local paper had announced that as a result of the prompt measures taken by the chief of police the situation was in hand. The Security Force would be kept mobilized, but as a precaution only, until it was clear that no further outrages were contemplated.

She looked down at the streets. Quite a few pedestrians were scurrying along between the swept piles of snow. A policeman stood at the corner directing traffic, the flaps of his cap pulled well down over his ears. It all looked peaceful enough.

In the consular office, Evelyn was saying to Charles, "The average Lienzer simply doesn't know what to make of it. The young Austrians are solidly behind Humbold. They're queuing to join

110

the Security Force. They are issued armbands and truncheons, and go round looking for people to hit on the head."

"It sounds like Berlin during a putsch."

"Or London during the general strike? Anyway, the arrest of Radler and Hammerle has shown people that Humbold means business. I don't think anyone knows quite how far he intends to go."

"Does he know himself?"

"I'm not sure. He could be a thoroughgoing Nazi-inspired, Pan-German fanatic, with backing from Munich and the Ruhr. There's an outfit in Munich which calls itself the Institute for Folk Culture and the Preservation of Historic Institutions in South Tyrol. They've got money to spare, most of it subscribed by Ruhr industrialists as a measure of tax evasion. This is the sort of lark they'd back to the hilt."

"Or else—?"

"Or he might just be mad."

The telephone rang, and Charles picked up the receiver. It was a one-sided conversation. After three or four minutes Charles managed to say, "I don't think I should do anything just yet. I'm going to try to get round to all our people this afternoon and this evening, to explain the situation to them."

"That was Colonel Crocker," he said. "He's one of our oldest residents. He tells me that he and his wife have a service rifle each, and a hundred and forty rounds of ammunition. He'd like to use them, too."

*   *   *

Charles had not reappeared by half past one, so Laura ate a solitary lunch. The snow had stopped falling, and the sky was like a damp, gray blanket. It looked close enough to touch.

"More snow this evening," said Frau Rosa. "Perhaps you will sleep this afternoon."

"There doesn't seem to be much else to do," Laura agreed. The radiators, now at full blast, had raised the temperature of the flat to an uncomfortable degree, and she had a headache. "I might lie down."

She was taking her shoes off when she heard the front doorbell ring; then the murmur of voices; then Frau Rosa knocked on the bedroom door.

"A visitor for you," she said.

Laura put her shoes on again, went out, and found Joe Keller in the drawing room.

"Am I glad to see you!" she said. "Did you have any difficulty getting in?"

"No difficulty getting in," said Joe. "That's the advantage of an apartment block. Anyone can slip in with the crowd."

"You were right, weren't you?"

"About what?"

"Your nose for trouble."

"Oh, that. I have to confess that that wasn't entirely intuition. We had a tip-off in Rome that there might be trouble when the Cardinal Bishop came down here. He was a hell-raiser all right, wasn't he?"

"He looked a very sincere man."

"It's the sincere men who are dangerous," said

Joe. "Give me insincerity and a quiet life."

"I should have thought this was just the sort of situation you reveled in."

"Ordinarily, yes. But there are circumstances here I hadn't taken into account."

"Such as?"

"Such as all the roads out being snowed up, the only available railroad track being blown up, and the wires being either cut or blocked, and the wireless under state control. You have to hand it to Colonel Julius. He got a security cordon round this state so quick—so goddam quick—you might have thought he'd got it all worked out in advance."

Laura had not been looking at him. Now she turned her head, and found his blue eyes on her, candid and guileless.

"I suppose," she said, "that he might have been expecting trouble—in a general sort of way, I mean."

"It's feasible," said Joe. "I don't believe it myself. But, then, no one pays much attention to what a newspaperman believes. By the way, would you care to tell me your story yourself?"

To her fury she felt the color creeping up her neck and cheeks.

"I didn't know it was public property."

"It's not as public as all that," said Joe. "I had to pay a lot of money to get hold of it. It's a good story. I'd say it'd be front-page news everywhere, if only we could get the damned thing out before it goes flat. What we really need's a carrier pigeon. A flock of pigeons. Did you actually *see* the gun?"

"Look here," said Laura, "I've been officially warned to keep my mouth shut. I've been unofficially deported. I'd be out of the country now if the railway was working. If I start making statements to the press, there really will be a row."

"I most solemnly promise you that you won't be quoted as an authority, at least not until you're clear of this country. And me too. That's a promise, Laura."

She was startled, for a moment, that he should have used her Christian name. Then she recollected that he was an American. She said, "Tell me how much you know already."

"The story is that you saw someone poke a gun out of a window in the theater, and time his shots so that he was covered by Boschetto. The big Italian was just a stalking horse. They needled him into waving his arms and shooting his gun off, but they knew he hadn't a hope in hell of hitting the right man. So they took care to have someone on the spot who would hit him."

"If you know that, you might as well know the rest," said Laura. "When I was getting away from the crowd I saw a man coming out of the theater. I'm as sure as I can be that he fired the shots."

"Know him to recognize him?"

"Certainly."

Joe pondered. "It's a great story," he said. "The greatest. It could even be true."

"What do you mean? Of course it's true."

"I was thinking of presentation," said Joe soothingly. "Not of essential veracity. A great newspaper story hasn't got to be actually true. It's got to seem possible." He reflected. "Once the idea got about that this was a Nazi-backed plot, people's minds would go right back to Van de Lubbe—the Reichstag fire—you remember?"

"I wasn't born when that happened. But I know what you mean. It's not quite as easy as that, though." She told him about the bullets.

"You *could* fake evidence like that," said Joe. "And I don't mean that you'd have to bribe all these professors. Not necessarily. Suppose you knew beforehand just what gun Boschetto was going to be carrying. He'd been in jail. All right. You know he's got a gun hidden somewhere. And you know that he'll go and pick it up as soon as he gets out. Maybe you have the place where he's hidden it under observation, to make sure he *does* pick it up."

"It's quite possible."

"But you've been there before him. You've had the gun out, fired two or three bullets through it, and preserved them. You bury two of them in the frontage of the theater."

"How do you know where?"

"You're organizing the parade. You know where the speaker's going to stand. He can't move away from the microphone."

"How do you know where Boschetto's going to be standing?"

"A certain amount of control would be needed there. My guess is, they got at his friends."

"If only someone else had seen the gun," said Laura.

"Someone else did," said Joe.

Laura said, "For goodness' sake—"

"Not a human eye. The eye of a camera. He was being photographed from half a dozen angles, remember. Cinecameras, ordinary cameras, telescopic lenses, the lot. I had maybe a couple of hundred negatives brought to my office immediately the show was over. They knew I'd give big money for a good one. Most of them were focused sharp on the speaker, but in one of them—it was one of the first batch I looked at—the focus had slipped. The Bishop was a blur—but there was lots of lovely sharp detail of the theater. I didn't look at it closely, because I hadn't heard your story, but I remember that one of the windows—it was the lowest window in the left-hand turret—it was open, a small way, at the top, and *something* was projecting."

Joe paused, his eyes shut and his mouth half open. He was visualizing the photograph.

"Boy," he said, and his voice had dropped almost to a whisper, "if we could get that photograph we could put it on every front page in the world."

"It might be an interesting exhibit at Boschetto's trial too."

"It might be that."

"Can you get hold of it?"

"I'm on the track. Luckily I wrote down the names of all the people who showed me photographs. I got them down in the order they arrived in my office. I know this was one of the first two or three batches. I'll have to do some leg work here. Everyone's scared of talking on the telephone."

"If you find it, what are you going to do with it?"

"I'll find some way of getting it out," said Joe. "Come to think of it, though, it mightn't be a bad idea if you were clear of the country *before* it appeared in the world's press."

"Curiously enough," said Laura, "the identical thought had already occurred to me."

Charles had had a busy afternoon. There were about forty English families in and around Lienz, and these he visited in turn, trailed by a Volkswagen containing two large young men in glasses. He found little alarm. The general view was that Humbold had overstepped the mark and that as soon as communications with Vienna had been restored he would be put in his place.

Colonel Crocker was not so sure. He and his wife, a small, fierce, yellow woman of sixty, had set up house together in many strange and unrestful corners of the globe.

"There's *something* brewing," said the Colonel. "I can smell it." Unlike Joe Keller, he had a nose which had evidently been constructed for smelling out trouble, a great, long, angled beak, with tufts of white hair sprouting from each nostril like smoke from the barrel of a revolver. "Last winter, when we had less snow than this, we were cut off

117

for six weeks. A madman can do a lot in six weeks."

"You think he's mad, Colonel?"

"Most foreigners are mad."

It was not the least trying part of a stiff afternoon and evening's work that each of the families he visited insisted on brewing him a cup of tea. It would have given offense to refuse it. By the time he reached home it was nearly seven o'clock. He was swilled and bloated with tea. He remembered reading in a medical journal that tea tasters often died, quite young, of kidney disease.

Outside the door of the block of flats a Fiat was parked which he recognized, through the gently swirling snow, as belonging to his Italian colleague, Dr. Pisoni. The doctor was at the wheel himself and looked reproachful.

"I have been waiting for you," he said.

"Was I meant to be meeting with you?"

"I spoke to a young man in your office."

"That would be Evelyn Fiennes."

"He sounded as if he was intoxicated."

"I don't think he'd be drunk quite as soon as that. And he couldn't have got hold of me anyway. I was moving around. What's up?"

"I sought permission to see the prisoner Boschetto. It has been granted."

"That's a step in the right direction."

"I would be very happy if you would come with me."

Charles sighed. What he desired at that moment, more than anything, was to take his sodden shoes off his aching feet, to put on his slippers, and to drink a glass of whisky. On the other hand, the half dozen members of the Diplomatic Corps in Lienz had a tradition of acting together in moments of crisis.

"All right," he said. "Where is he?"

"At police headquarters, in the Greitestrasse. Leave your car here, if you like. I will drive you."

As the cell door was opened by the policeman, and Inspector Moll showed them in, Charles had in his mind various images of political prisoners—emaciated men, with straggling beards, chained to walls. What he was not prepared for was a normal-looking, apparently contented Italian, eating a dish of pasta, with a mug of wine beside his plate.

Boschetto raised his eyes when they came in, but he did not get up, nor did he discontinue his eating.

Dr. Pisoni spoke to him in Italian. Charles had a serviceable knowledge of the language and could follow the opening exchanges. Yes, Boschetto had been well treated after he had been rescued from the crowd. He agreed that he had been carrying a gun—for his own protection. Many people in Austria did the same. Yes, he had heard about the death of his brother. (And seemed, Charles thought, singularly unmoved by the news.) No, he had no complaints. He had been informed that his trial would take place in a few days' times. Yes, he had been given a lawyer to help him prepare his defense. He mentioned the name, Professor Ciresa, and Dr. Pisoni nodded approvingly. The professor, himself a South Tyrolese, he explained to Charles, was a well-known jurist and would certainly do his best for the prisoner.

At the end Boschetto said something in rapid Italian. Dr. Pisoni looked surprised, and said something back which Charles again missed.

"I didn't get that."

"He says that Professor Ciresa has advised him to speak with complete frankness. He says that it will be his best chance."

"I suppose so."

"Particularly, he should be frank about his accomplice."

"Had he an accomplice?"

Dr. Pisoni put the question. A long pause ensued. The prisoner's embarrassment was evident. Then Charles caught Boschetto looking at him out of the corner of his eye, and realized that it was his presence that was troubling him.

Dr. Pisoni said, "I think he does not want to answer that question."

9

Laura Has a
Night Out

IN HER SECOND TO LAST REPORT on Laura (not the
final one; that was always conceived in terms of
kindly optimism) Miss Sennett had written:
"Sometimes she thinks before she acts. Sometimes
she does not." After a gap, which indicated a pause
in her thoughts, she had added, in her neat hand-
writing: "I do not really know which is the more
dangerous."

On this occasion Miss Sennett could not have
accused Laura of lack of thought. She thought
hard, weighing the displeasure of her brother
against the delights of a night out with so accom-
plished a host as Helmut. She thought long; from
half past four, when Frau Rosa brought in tea in a
flowered china teapot and savory toast in a plated
dish, until half past seven, when there was still no
sign of Charles.

If he isn't back by a quarter to eight—she

thought. And then, If he isn't back by eight o'clock—

At ten past eight she scribbled on a piece of paper: "I am having dinner with Helmut, at the Elisabeth in Rudolf-Strasse. Don't worry about me. I'll be home in good time."

Then she collected her coat and hat and started to explain things to Frau Rosa.

The old lady grasped the essentials.

"You are going out to dinner."

"That's right. You remember the gentleman who was here the first night—"

"With a young man."

"He isn't really very young."

"You will eat good food at the Elisabeth. The cook is French."

"Lovely," said Laura. "See, I've left a note for my brother. What I wanted to know was if you could show me the back way out. You remember what you said this morning. The dentist—"

This took a little more putting across, but Frau Rosa got there in the end. Not for nothing had she served as housekeeper to four successive bachelor vice-consuls.

"You are dining with a young man, and you do not wish the police to know. I will get my key."

It was not at all plain to Laura why Frau Rosa should have a key to the dentist's office on the ground floor, but she undoubtedly had one. And a few minutes later they were crossing the room. The chair was swathed in a white sheet, the dread instruments locked away in a steel-and-glass cabinet. The kitchen door was only bolted. It opened onto a tiny, empty courtyard containing a fig tree and walled on three sides.

A farther door was unlocked. Beyond it lay a similar courtyard, but this one was crammed with crates, boxes, cartons, and bottles. From beyond a lighted entrance came a clatter of voices.

"We go through here," said Frau Rosa, and before Laura could protest she found herself in a crowded kitchen. Frau Rosa waved to one of the women and walked straight through. Laura thought that the occupants of the room looked at her curiously, but no one spoke to her. The next minute she was in the foyer of a restaurant.

"Very simple," said Frau Rosa. "For the police I have contempt."

Helmut was waiting for her inside the door of the Elisabeth. He removed her coat, handed it to a waiter, and led the way to a table. She saw at once that Helmut was a good person to go out dining with. If he had owned the Elisabeth, its staff could not have jumped more smoothly to his bidding.

"I hope you are going to like this," he said. "With some girls I should not have dared. They would have turned up their noses at anything but gin."

"What is it?"

"It is Chambéry. A French vermouth. It comes from the foothills of the Alps."

It was pale, pale yellow, the color of a young girl's hair; and as cold as a young girl's heart. It did not taste alcoholic.

"I am glad that you were able to get away to-night," said Helmut. "I feared very much that your brother might forbid it."

"I haven't seen him since breakfast time," said Laura. "I don't see why he should object, do you?"

"It is true that the situation has become much calmer. As long as the people feel that their leaders are taking decisive action on their behalf, they will not be restive."

"And do they feel that?"

"Certainly. I do not think that his worst enemy could accuse Hofrat Humbold of lack of drive."

"He's got drive all right. The thing is, where is he driving to?"

"I don't imagine that anyone could answer that, except the Hofrat himself. And, possibly, Colonel Schatzmann."

There was an undercurrent in Helmut's voice. An enthusiasm which he tried carefully to keep under control. Laura said, "Is it true that you are a member of the Berg Isel Bund?"

For a moment she thought she had gone too far. Then Helmut smiled slowly.

"Yes," he said. "It is true. I have long been a member. How did you know?"

"Joe told me."

"Joe?"

"His name's Joe Keller; he's American."

"The newspaperman. Yes." Helmut waved his hand, and the waiter refilled their glasses. "He is one of those Americans with baby faces. Big, blue eyes, and a little-boy nose. I must warn you. They are very dangerous. Where did you meet him?"

"In Rome, actually."

"I see. We must finish our drinks, or it is possible we will lose our table."

"Aren't we eating here?"

"Certainly not. The chef here has only one idea. To smother everything with French sauce. We are going to a place where you can taste the food. It is not very far from here. It is called Mousie's."

Mousie's was delightful. It was a single room, at the back of the first floor of what looked like a delicatessen store. The room held six tables. They stood around the wall, so that each one had a broad, cushioned sofa at one side, and chairs on the sides. Laura wondered if they were going to share the sofa, but Helmut conducted her to it, and seated himself at the other side of the table.

She found that he had no intention of consulting her as to food or drink. Everything had been arranged in advance. Except that it looked plain, and tasted delightful, Laura had no very clear recollection of what she ate, but she did remember the wine. This was brought up in a padded leather carrier by a tiny, old, humpbacked man. (Mousie himself?) It was a larger bottle than she had ever seen at close quarters before.

"I may have said harsh things about French food," said Helmut, as the gnome uncorked the bottle, "but it would be affectation to despise their wines. Taste it before you talk about it."

It tasted perfect. Softer than the Chambéry, but

not sweet; indeed, it had a resinous tang which touched the back of her throat as a man's hand will touch, for a fraction of a second, the hand of a woman he desires.

She knew that she had never drunk wine like it before, and she was sensible enough to realize that it was a waste of words for her to praise it.

"Lovely," she said. "What is it?"

"You are drinking a Clos-Blanc de Vougeot. The red Vougeot is a good, reliable wine. The white is exceptional. This is only twelve years old, but twelve is a great age for a white Burgundy. Finish what was put in your glass, and Carl will fill it for you."

Later the talk shifted from wine to women.

"It seems to me," said Helmut, "that English girls suffer from one great disadvantage."

"What is that, Helmut?"

"I refer to their mothers. Cast your mind back. What were the lessons your mother instilled in you?"

Laura considered the matter, her head cocked a fraction to one side. The wine was circulating inside her, loosening strings, undoing knots which had been tied before.

"She was very strong on good manners. She hated anyone's being late for meals. She liked me to brush my teeth three times a day."

"Nothing more?"

"She wasn't terribly keen on education, but she saw that I went to the right sort of boarding school

—the sort where one did riding and classical dancing."

"And the mistresses at that school, they continued your mother's teaching—manners, punctuality, and clean teeth?"

"I suppose they did, really, yes."

"And neither your mother nor any of these wise teachers taught you the only thing that matters. That a girl should be made ready for love."

In ordinary circumstances a remark like this would have knocked Laura off balance. Now, she simply tilted her head the other way, focused her eyes on the soft brown ones opposite her, and said, "Helmut, you're exaggerating."

"I assure you I am not. No French, no Italian or Spanish mother would think otherwise. And since many Europeans go to America, I fancy that American mothers are beginning to think the same. It is only the Anglo-Saxons who still bring girls up as if they were boys."

"What do you mean *exactly*—made ready for love?"

"I mean that a girl should be taught that she has been given a body for two purposes—for making love and bearing children. That is the biological position. Civilization has added complications. Marriage, for example, is an extra."

"Like ballet dancing, and milk after supper."

"Like?— I see. Your mind is still at school. There are, of course, women who have never made love. They are to be pitied. Like children born with one arm."

At that moment the table seemed to Laura to be a barrier. It was too wide. It was getting in the way of the most exciting talk she could ever remember.

"Couldn't you come and sit beside me?" she said.

"I could do so," said Helmut. The wine seemed to have had no effect on him at all. His face was unflushed, his speech was precise. "But I fear that it is too narrow to accommodate both of us. And it would cause a comment. Instead we will go dancing."

"Dancing?"

"Only if you would like to."

"I'd love it."

The bill got itself paid, or waved away. Laura got up cautiously. Her coat was found. And they were outside.

The street was cold and empty. The snow had stopped falling and the sky, for the first time in two days, was clear. A thousand diamonds, a million specks of diamond dust, glittered on black velvet. Her heart rose to greet them. How right she had been to come!

There was ice on the pavement, and Helmut put his hand on her arm to guide her to the car. It was an awkward car to get into but, once in, it fitted you like a second skin.

There was ice on the roads too: ice and patches of packed, frozen snow. Helmut drove with delicate precision. The first time they struck a patch of ice she drew her breath in sharply as, instead of slowing, he increased his speed, turning into the front wheel skid and correcting it at the last moment.

He heard her gasp and said, "I apologize. I am showing off. But it is quite safe, as long as the roads are empty. There is not likely to be much traffic on a night like this."

"Where are we going?"

"It is called the Winterhaus. It is about five kilometers outside Lienz, on the lake. It is a private club for people with the same enthusiasms. Sailing in summer and skiing in winter."

"It sounds lovely."

"It is a very big house, and extremely ugly. It was built by an Austrian millionaire, fifty years ago, as a residence for his Hungarian mistress. She took one look at the house, and returned to Hungary. Then it stood empty for many years. Here is the driveway."

"I see what you mean," said Laura. "It doesn't look *too* bad."

"You should see it by daylight."

The door was opened for them by a massive figure. Under the shaded lights Laura could not make out, for a moment, whether it was a man or a woman; then she saw that it was, in fact, a middle-aged woman, with iron-gray hair, and the solid, square-standing, chest forward, backside-out figure of a regimental sergeant major in the Brigade of Guards.

"Guten Abend, Tante Margarete," said Helmut.

The woman said something in Austrian too rapid for Laura. She gathered that Aunt Margaret was reporting on the evening's proceedings. Helmut nodded and said, "Good, good."

As the lady advanced and took her wrap, Laura was aware of a close and analytical scrutiny. It brought an elusive memory back to her. It was, she thought, the look which a doctor gives his patient as he removes his coat.

She said to Helmut, "What an extraordinary woman."

"Without her there would be no club," said Helmut. He was guiding her between the dozen tables that fringed that side of a small dance floor. "And that would be a pity, for I know of few better clubs than this."

It was a big room, the drawing room and dining room of the original owner, leading out at the far end onto a broad terrace, now sealed by double glass windows. The walls from the squared roof beams to the polished wood of the floor were tapestry covered.

"This is our table. You will find the service here good. We have the best waiters in Europe."

For the first time that evening a note of real warmth had crept into his tone. It was for a second only. Then his guard was up again.

"I should think," she said, "that they must all be scared stiff of Aunt Marge."

The waiter who was now standing beside them looked no more than eighteen. He had a smooth, brown face and light-brown hair, and moved like a dancer.

"I am at a loss," said Helmut, "to know what to

suggest. We have liqueurs of a sort, I believe. Truly, after such a wine, we should drink brandy. But it may be a drink you do not care for at all."

"I think brandy would be lovely."

"Then, Albin, we will have two glasses of brandy. That one, I think. Two large glasses."

As the boy bent his head over the wine list the light glinted on the soft down on the edge of his chin. Eighteen? He could hardly be more than sixteen.

A voice at the next table claimed her attention. A man was speaking in the hard German of the North. This was one straight out of the book, thought Laura. He had small, shrewd eyes, deep set in a huge, almost hairless head, large enough to overbalance his body, had not nature thoughtfully provided him with a neck thick enough to support it without danger; a neck, indeed, so thick that it was difficult to see where neck ended and head began.

"Like a clothes-peg man," said Laura.

"I beg your pardon."

"I can't explain."

"Shall we dance while we are waiting for the drinks?"

"Yes," said Laura. "Let's do that."

When he touches me, she thought, I shall find out. Helmut took her right hand in his left, put his other hand in the small of her back, and steered her expertly across the floor. There was as much passion in it as a professional dancing master with his twelfth pupil since lunch.

The terminals had touched, but there was no current.

After one dance she said, "Shall we go back and sit down now?" and Helmut conducted her politely to their table.

The brandy had arrived, and Laura picked up her glass, and emptied almost half of it down her throat. She had to do something to stop herself crying.

Helmut was saying something, in his courteous, level voice, but she was not listening. Her glass was empty. Helmut signaled, and Albin came up again. His smile, thought Laura, was most attractive. When he opened his lips he had small, strong teeth like pearls.

"I can see," said Helmut, "that you liked your brandy. Might I suggest a further glass?"

"Thank you. I'd like that."

Her voice was surprisingly steady. She was very nearly drunk, but one part of her mind, one lobe of her brain which the alcohol had not reached, was functioning with great clarity. She noticed, for instance, that there was a door in the tapestry on the wall, not far from their table. The handle was countersunk into the tapestry. She was curious about this door. At one moment, it opened inward for a fraction, as if someone behind it was surveying the room. Then it closed again.

The table next to theirs, where the clothes-peg man had sat, was deserted; but the brandy glass on it had been refilled. Odd, thought the still observant part of Laura. He didn't look like a man who would leave a drink.

She turned to say so to Helmut, when she found that, for the first time that evening, his attention was not on her. He was listening to the sounds from the front hall. A man was shouting, in English. And Laura had a feeling that she recognized the voice.

"If you will excuse me for one moment," said Helmut. As he got to his feet there was a crash from the hall, and Helmut started to run.

Without any clear reasoning to prompt her, Laura had got up too. All eyes were on the fracas in the front hall, which was growing. At least three people were shouting now. She took a quick step across to the tapestry, pushed open the door, and went through. The door shut quietly behind her on a counterweight.

It was a bare passage. At the end of it was a short flight of stairs which invited her to climb them. She went up, and found she was in a corridor, running at right angles to the one she had quitted. There were numbered doors on either side and a window at the end. She thought a bit about this, decided that perhaps she had come far enough, and then thought, Why not? Probably the doors were all locked, anyway. She turned a handle at random and looked in.

It was a curious sort of room, dimly lit from a cornice light, and bare of anything in the nature of ordinary furniture. At the far end, however, stood an odd-looking instrument with eyepieces, mounted on a tripod and facing the blank wall. If it had been set up at a window it might have been some sort of telescope.

She walked across and put her eyes to the eyepieces. She found herself looking, at very close quarters, at the empty chair she had left five minutes before. As she watched, half of Helmut came back into focus. He seemed bothered about something, and spoke to a pair of legs. Laura touched the eyepieces and found that they pivoted freely on a sort of gimbals. They were very high-powered, fixed-focus lenses.

She trained them around the room. The effect was extraordinary. The least movement blurred the scene. But as soon as the instrument came to rest, a very high-definition picture of a very small part of the room appeared.

This time she was looking at a lady of about forty in an extremely low-cut evening dress. Indeed, viewed from this particular angle, it was cut so low that it might not have been there at all, for any useful purpose it was serving. The focus was so fine that she could see a drop of sweat gathered between the lady's breasts. She touched the glasses gently, and nearly cried out.

She was staring, at the closest possible quarters, at the murderer of the Cardinal Bishop.

She straightened up. Get help of some sort. Tell somebody. Do something. Go back to Helmut. He would know what to do.

She had almost reached the top of the stairs when she heard footsteps coming up.

She turned, in panic, and pulled open the nearest door.

A great, white furious face glared at her. She had just time to recognize the clothes-peg man. Someone screamed out an oath. She jumped back into the passage, and slammed the door.

It was Albin who had been coming up the stairs, and now he stood, smiling curiously at her.

Laura muttered something, and tried to brush past him. An arm slid round her waist, and Albin said, "What are you doing up here?" His voice was husky.

"Lost my way," said Laura. She, too, was whispering. "Let me go. Please."

Albin's face was very close to hers. There was a curious light in the brown eyes. The mouth, close to hers, was half open and the little tongue flicked between the lips.

"I will find a room."

It was only then that she realized that Albin was not a boy at all. She was being held by a girl, and there was nothing innocent in the eyes looking into hers. For the next few moments events took on the quality of a nightmare. All movements were difficult. Sequence was disconnected. Impressions formed quickly, but dissolved slowly.

The girl who had hold of her was older and stronger than she was. Over her shoulder she saw, without much surprise, that the passage window was open, and that a man was climbing through it. One of the girl's arms was pinioning her, the other was pulling the front of her dress. The man was in the passage now and was coming softly toward them. She recognized Evelyn Fiennes. The girl who was holding her either heard him or, more probably, felt the draft from the open window. She turned her head, but without releasing Laura. This was a mistake. It made her very vulnerable to attack. Evelyn started to tickle her.

Albin screamed, and let go of Laura. Evelyn picked her up in both arms, a feat he could barely manage, for the girl was almost as big as he was, and said, "Open the door, quick." He was nodding toward the room on her right.

She opened it, and heard a second scream of rage from the fat man. Then Evelyn had thrown the girl in, and slammed the door.

"Out the window. Don't dither. It's not a long drop."

When she was halfway through, he pushed her, and she found herself on her knees in the snow. She gave a yelp as Evelyn landed beside her, one foot on her hand.

"Sorry," he said. "Into the car."

"I'm going to be sick."

"There's no time. They'll be round here in a minute."

His old Austin, which she recognized, was parked on a rockery. It seemed an odd place to put a car. Evelyn was already climbing into the driving seat, and she staggered round to the other side and tumbled in beside him.

He put his left arm round her to slam the door while his right hand was engaging first gear. With a double jerk, which first threw her almost into the back seat and then banged her against the windshield, the car shot forward, scuttered through a snowdrift, and slid onto the frozen front drive.

In front of the house were signs of activity. The front door was open. One man was standing on the steps and another was in one of the parked cars, trying to start the engine.

This seemed to remind Evelyn of something. He dipped his right hand into his coat pocket and pulled out a small bag, which he threw at the man on the steps. For a moment Laura thought it might be some sort of bomb, but the bag fell softly onto the snow, and nothing else happened. Then they were in the front drive, gathering speed.

As a driver, Evelyn wasn't in Helmut's class. When he went into a skid he started swearing, and went on swearing until the car righted itself. Twice they went off the drive altogether, on the second occasion slicing through a small hedge and carrying away part of it on their radiator.

"Camouflage," said Evelyn. At the gate he turned left.

"The town's the other way, beside the lake."

"Certainly. And if you'd kept your eyes open you'd have seen two sets of headlights coming along the lake road. I can't help feeling they're unfriendly."

"What could they do?"

"Arrest me for drunken driving, for a start," said Evelyn.

In the stuffy proximity of the car she could

smell the whisky on his breath.

"Where *does* this road go?"

"Up the mountain. There's a sort of side road off that goes back to town. If I can find it. And if it isn't blocked by snow."

"Now I *am* going to be sick."

"Out the window. Not over me."

"Couldn't you stop? Just for a minute?"

"If I did, I shouldn't get started again. Not on this gradient."

"What was it you threw at him?"

"At whom?"

"The man on the steps."

"The distributor arms out of six of the eight cars. I couldn't get the other two. The bonnets were locked. It'll take them some time to find out which is which."

"Was it you making a row in the hall?"

"It was. And they threw me out."

"Then how did you get to that window?"

"You do nothing but ask questions."

"Asking questions stops me wanting to be sick."

"What an odd constitution you must have. When they'd slung me out, I drove away down the drive with my lights on, and came back across the lawn with my lights off. It's as well to keep these things simple. Here we go."

He swung the car into what looked like a snow-bank. The wheels threshed as its momentum carried it up the first, steep slope, then it was on level, frozen road, bouncing and skidding.

"Downhill now. Should do it," said Evelyn.

The car ran into a slight depression, and the engine stalled.

"Damn and blast you, you stinking old cow," said Evelyn to the car. "What did you want to do that for? So nearly there too." And to Laura, "Here's where you get out and push."

"I don't think I can."

"It's that or freeze to death."

Somehow she dragged herself out. She pushed, slipped, sobbed, and moaned. At the last moment, when she was about to give up and lie down in the snow, the wildly rotating wheels gripped and the car pulled itself, by its bootstraps, to the top of the little depression.

"Run," said Evelyn. "Daren't stop. Jump."

Then she was inside again. Oddly, she no longer felt sick. The car gathered speed, bumping on the frozen surface, slithering somehow through the softer drifts.

"Hit the main road any minute now," said Evelyn. "Hit something, anyway," he added, as the car splintered what seemed to be a light pole across the road and came, for a second time, to a stop.

"One more push."

Laura climbed out, then put her head in again. "We're on a railway," she said.

"I thought we hit something."

Evelyn climbed out, too, and walked forward a few yards. A second, counterweighted pole stretched across their path. For this very secondary road and branch line it was evidently considered a sufficient barrier.

"I'd better get this up. No need to do unnecessary damage. It's probably got some sort of trick catch. Give me the torch from the glove compartment, would you?"

"Evelyn."

"Yes. What is it?"

"You don't think there's any chance a train might be coming, do you?"

"Most unlikely. This is only a branch line."

"Then what's that noise?"

Evelyn stopped fiddling with the pole, raised his head, and said, "My God, I believe you're right." He looked at the car, and said, "No, I'm damned if I'm going to leave the old cow." He stepped back, and kicked at the pole. The second kick broke the catch which he had been unable to unfasten. The pole swung up.

Blowing sparks from its funnel, a freight engine came with majestic slowness round the curve. It seemed to be towing flatcars loaded with logs.

Evelyn jumped into the driving seat, Laura jumped in beside him. He started the engine and slammed in the gear. After a breath-taking hesitation, the old car gathered herself together and shot off the railway line. The engine was still a full hundred yards away.

"What the hell did you want to get back in the car for?" said Evelyn, as they ran out onto the Lienz road.

"I wasn't thinking," said Laura. "It all happened so suddenly."

"It's when things happen suddenly," said Evelyn, "that you need to think."

Ten minutes later they reached the flat. The watchers in the doorway stirred, and stamped their feet, but did nothing. They had no instructions about people going in.

An anxious Charles was waiting for them in the ground-floor lobby.

"I thought I heard your car arrive," he said. "It's nearly four o'clock. What have you been up to?"

"Nothing, really," said Laura. Her feet slipped on the polished floor and she fell flat on her face.

10

Hangover

"I SUPPOSE I OUGHT TO BE GRATEFUL to you," said Laura.

It was eleven o'clock on the following morning. Her head ached, her mouth was full of grit. Her body felt as if it had been passed through a tight mangle.

"There's no actual rule about it," said Evelyn. "Some people do feel grateful when they've been saved from making thundering asses of themselves. Mostly they don't."

"How was I to know Helmut was on their side?"

"You first met him when Humbold brought him to dinner here, didn't you?"

"Yes, but—"

"And you knew he was an active member of the Berg Isel Bund, didn't you?"

"Yes."

"Then whose side did you expect him to be on?"

"He seemed rather nice at first." Aware that this

sounded feeble, Laura added, "In fact, just the sort of man a girl *does* like to be taken out by."

"It depends on the girl."

"What do you mean by that?"

"I should have thought even you would have realized by now that he was a screaming pansy."

"Well—yes—I think I did at the end. When we were dancing together."

"He's got boy friends in half the capitals of Europe."

"You're exaggerating."

"I'm certainly not exaggerating. He's notorious for it. His ski team members were chosen almost entirely for their good looks. The other competitors used to call them Helmut and his Angels."

"I don't believe it."

"And another thing. Do you know who his current boy friend in Lienz is?"

"Of course I don't."

"Well, it's your pal Hans."

"Hans who?"

"Hans Dorf. Baby-face. The chap you saw coming out of the theater. He isn't a Tyrolese at all, incidentally. He comes from Munich."

Laura said crossly, "*If* you knew all this, why didn't you stop me going out with Helmut?"

"Because you never consulted me."

She felt that he was being unfair, without being able to say exactly how.

"Anyway," she said, "I still don't see what the object was. If he didn't want me, why did he take me out?"

"Try using those small pieces of cosmic jelly sometimes loosely referred to as your brain," said Evelyn. "You represent a danger to the state. The state, just at this moment and until the snow melts, is Hofrat Humbold and Colonel Schatzmann. They have gone to a lot of trouble to produce a certain situation. An important part of the setup is that Boschetto should be guilty of murder. His trial starts in two days' time. Then, out of the blue, a witness—a highly inconvenient witness—turns up. And threatens to give evidence against them."

Evelyn paused to stub out one cigarette and light another. Laura said nothing. She had nothing to say. In the gray light of morning, under a leaden sky, the situation which had seemed exciting, even amusing, had for a moment shown its true face. She felt in her stomach a sickness which was not entirely a legacy of the previous evening. She wished that she was a thousand miles away. She wished she was back in Rome. She was afraid.

"In the old days," said Evelyn, "you wouldn't have presented any problem to anyone. You would have been dropped into an oubliette and left there until people had forgotten about you. In this day and age these things aren't so easy. There is the press. There is the UN. There is the national conscience. If a witness threatens to be inconvenient nowadays, the authorities can't put him into an iron mask. But there are steps they can take. Other, rather more subtle, steps. They can discredit him."

144

"And that was the object of last night's maneuvers."

"Of course."

"What was it—that awful place?"

"I can't think of a single word for it," said Evelyn. "It's a pale carbon copy of the notorious Green House outside Berlin."

The name stirred a faint memory. It was something an elderly diplomat had once said to Charles; some sort of masculine joke.

"The German Secret Service thought it up. It's said to have had its origin at a time when they wanted to blackmail the Spanish Ambassador. He had—very peculiar tastes. They arranged to gratify them. And they recorded some of the more sensational moments with a concealed camera. It proved so successful that they extended it. Almost every perversion was catered to—and recorded. Sometimes the object was blackmail. Sometimes it was rather more subtle. Know your enemy and exploit his weaknesses. That sort of thing."

"It's just the sort of disgusting thing the Nazis would think up."

"You can't blame the Nazis for this one. The Green House was Bismarck's idea."

"Were *all* the waiters girls?"

"I shouldn't think all of them, no."

"What was meant to happen to me?"

"It depended how tight they got you. You'd have ended up in one of those little upstairs rooms."

"I wouldn't have gone quietly, I promise you that."

"The harder you'd fought," said Evelyn, "the more interesting the photographs would have been."

Laura thought about this for a moment, and then said, "How did you know where I'd gone?"

"I bought the information. There's nothing you can't buy if you offer the right price. By the way, did you see that fat German—the one in the room where I shoved that waiter—"

"I saw him earlier on."

"Did you recognize him?"

"Should I have?"

"You might have seen his picture in the papers. He's Baron Buschli. He was Minister for Agricultural Development in the West German government. Then he resigned his post to become head man in a very curious setup which calls itself the Institute for Rural and Cultural Studies. It's a sort of cover name for a section of the Pan-Germanic party."

Evelyn added, "Come to think of it, the Baron was going in for some pretty intensive cultural studies last night, wasn't he? All the same, I'd rather deal with someone plain nasty like Buschli than someone cold crazy like Humbold."

Joe Keller, who had called on Laura after lunch, said much the same thing. "There's nothing nastier," he said, "than when a ruler, or someone who's temporarily in the position of a ruler, seems to be losing his head. When I say that, I don't mean behaving rashly. I mean behaving madly. When he starts doing things that would get an ordinary citizen locked up."

"It can't last long," said Laura. "As soon as the passes are open, they'll bring him back to his senses."

"As soon as— That's what people used to say about Hitler. As soon as he goes into the Ruhr, France will bring him to heel. As soon as he touches Czechoslovakia, the world will be up in arms. What you don't realize is that people here are still pretty primitive. And they're right behind Humbold. A lot of them have got relatives in the South Tyrol. The difficulty was getting them started. I don't know if you've ever studied chemistry?"

"Chemistry," said Laura, "is one of lots of things I know nothing about."

"I don't know a lot myself. But here's something anyone who owns a car will understand: To create an explosion, you need two things. The first is compression. The second is a spark. You got your compression when Lienz was cut off from the rest of the world."

"And the killing was the spark."

"That's right. And that's what's making them so sore at you. Did you notice they'd doubled the guard?"

"I hadn't looked."

"You've got half a dozen men out there now. And they've got a field telephone, so they can call up reinforcements pretty quick."

"They didn't stop you coming in."

147

"I don't think they're there to stop people coming in and out. Their primary job is to protect you."

Laura looked at him blankly.

"I don't suppose you realize quite how far this has gone," said Joe. "But, getting about as I do, I hear things. People are beginning to get a bit worked up about you. What they want to do is shoot Boschetto and march into the Tyrol. In that order. Only you're standing in the way of step number one."

Laura said, "I haven't done anything yet. No one's even asked me to give evidence." She disliked herself as she said it.

"The trouble is, such a lot of people have heard your story it's going to look pretty funny if you *don't* give evidence now."

Laura contemplated the future glumly. "I'm beginning to wish I'd never come here," she said.

"I wouldn't go along with that," said Joe. "If you hadn't come, I should never have had the pleasure of meeting you."

"Thank you, Joe."

"All the same, I think it might be a sound idea, taken all round, if your brother made arrangements to evacuate you in the fairly near future."

"You think it's as bad as that?"

Joe said, with a careful lack of expression which Laura had begun to recognize, "I should say that, however bad things are now, they would be bound to get worse when the American and European papers start featuring my story."

148

"You've managed to get it past the censor?"

"Not yet. No. I'm planning to take it out personally."

"You mean *my* story."

"I mean your story, yes."

"Will people believe it? Will they publish it?"

"They'll believe it and publish it when they see the photograph."

"You've got it?"

"I'm near to it. It was taken by a local photographer called Hoffracker. I guess he knew he was onto something good. It's costing me five hundred pounds. I had to get hold of the money in Swiss currency before he'd part with it."

"Why Swiss?"

"I can only surmise," said Joe, "that Hoffracker plans to be in Switzerland himself when the story breaks."

He added, "I feel that way too, Laura." He put his right hand around her shoulders and, as she opened her mouth in surprise, kissed her once, warmly, expertly, and with considerable passion.

Then he was gone. Laura heard the front door bang. She said, out loud, "Well, that made a nice change, anyway."

11

Joe Gets to Hell
Out of It

FOR HIS WORK Joe borrowed a room from the Trans-World Press Agency, which kept an office on the fourth floor of a block on the Adelbodener-Strasse.

Normally, what happened in Lienz was of little interest to the world at large, and the local T.W.P.A. representative, a genial Carinthian called Sandholzner, had plenty of time to pursue his other activities. This was lucky, for he was a much occupied man. He was consular representative in Lienz of three Baltic states, gave advice on tax evasion, and edited a magazine devoted to joinery and fretwork.

He raised his bald head as Joe came in and regarded him benevolently. Joe seemed to him to represent the great outside world: the world where things happened, where important decisions were taken, where fortunes and reputations were made;

a world which Herr Sandholzner was heartily glad to be out of.

"I hope your affairs prosper," he said.

"So-so," said Joe. "In one way I'm getting on, in another way I'm slipping back."

"That is life."

"Look," said Joe, "you know this country a lot better than I do. If you had to get out of it—on your own—which way would you go?"

"When you say 'on your own' do you mean without troubling the customs authorities or without troubling the police?"

"Without troubling anyone at all."

Herr Sandholzner considered the matter. "Some years ago," he said, "when I was interested in the collection of wildflowers—I had a project at that time for a magazine devoted to wildflower collection—each month we would have had a different wildflower pressed between the pages. Unfortunately the project proved too expensive—"

"You were saying—?"

"Yes. In the course of collecting specimens I wandered quite freely in the Lienz Dolomites. They form the frontier with Italy."

"I've got a map here if it will help."

"I must get my glasses. Yes. That line of alternate dots and dashes is the international boundary. It runs along the line of peaks. The controls are in the valley, on each side."

"Is the frontier anything at all—when you get there?"

"Is there a fence, you mean? Certainly not.

151

There are perhaps stones, surveyors' marks. Nothing more. I have wandered many times into Italy without knowing it. And back again."

"But that was in summer."

"In spring—summer—autumn. There is little or no snow. Now it would not be so easy. You could cross on foot, without doubt, at the western end. The mountains there are not high. But there you are in the zone of frontier control."

"Whereas," said Joe, "if I keep south and east I keep clear of the controls, but it becomes a stiff climb. Right?"

"There is no climbing in the true sense of the word; nothing for which you would need a rope or an ax. But certain parts of the journey would be easier on skis."

"That's all right."

"You are adept?"

"I can get by," said Joe.

"Have you got a car?"

"I've got a rented car."

"Strap your skis to the roof. Many young people out for a day's skiing do the same. They will serve as a passport for you."

"Good idea," said Joe. "Double bluff."

"Then what I suggest you do is this: Take your car down the road toward Sillian, but turn to your left before you get there. Look, I will show you on the map. It is a very small road, which turns off just past Abfaltersbach. It crosses the River Drava and climbs at once. It will undoubtedly be blocked by snow, but the first part of it may be clear. You could leave your car here—or here. Hide it in a barn, if you can find one. That will delay inquiry. Then go straight up the side of the mountain. You have used skins under your skis before?"

"Surely."

"Then it should not be too difficult. Go quite openly. People who see you will imagine you are climbing up for a run down. All you have to do is to keep the Kreuzberg—Monte Croce, as the Italians call it—on your left. With luck you will be in Italy in two hours."

"With luck," said Joe soberly. On the small-scale map the distance looked quite manageable. There was a peak marked some way to the left of his crossing place, 2,678 meters. Joe did some mental arithmetic. That would be over eight thousand feet. Too high for a novice in midwinter.

As he was going, Herr Sandholzner said, "Do you know a small boy with light hair and a squint?"

"I don't think so. Why?"

"There was one here this morning, very early, asking for you."

"Did he say what he wanted?"

"No. But he said it was urgent."

"If he turns up again," said Joe, "give him a couple of schillings and tell him I'll be back in an hour."

Herr Hoffracker had his shop and studio in a small street in the Oberlienz suburb, on the hillside to the north of the town. Joe took the tram to the foot of the hill and then climbed the street, which ran up between the terraced houses and shops. The sun was out and the sky was blue, but it was filmed with wisps of lacy cloud which were being chased across it by some high-altitude wind.

The entrance to the shop was down three steps from the pavement. It was a small, dark, mean-looking place. Through the misted front window a selection of wedding photographs was visible, the girls in white, the men wearing the look of glazed complacency common to bridegrooms and anglers who have landed an exceptional fish.

Joe pushed open the door and went in. The bell on the door went ting-tang but no one came in answer to his summons.

On the counter was a placard, in ornate script, which Joe spent some minutes translating. It seemed to say: "Of the happiest moment of your life a visible monument create."

Gosh, but it was warm! The little room felt like an oven. Somebody had certainly got the central heating going.

Joe rang the bell again, took out a handkerchief, and wiped the sweat from his forehead. The silence grew oppressive. He rang the bell loudly three or four times and walked across to the back of the shop. Apart from the street entrance there was only one possible way in or out, and that was a door beyond the end of the counter, which led to some sort of room at the back.

Joe knocked, got no answer, turned the handle, and opened the door. It did not come easily. It was as if it had warped in its frame. He put his

154

shoulder to it and it moved sluggishly back.

The heat hit him in the face. The room inside was in darkness, but he could see that an enormous fire had been built in the wall stove. It was glowing and pulsing, overflowing the stove. There was a pile of red-hot stuff on the brickwork.

In a sudden panic Joe felt for the wall switch and pressed it down. Under the big neon lights the room jumped out to meet him. It was a studio. In the middle stood a camera, with a chair and screens in front of it. In the corner was a sink. Round the wall ran slatted shelves which must once have contained materials, spare film, prints, and mounts. They were now empty. Someone had stripped everything off them, every photograph, every negative, and every film, had stuffed it all into the stove and set fire to it. Whoever did it, thought Joe, must have managed it pretty carefully not to set himself and the house on fire.

The only other piece of furniture in the room was a filing cabinet. He walked across and pulled the drawers open, but it was only a gesture. He knew before he looked that the cabinet would be as empty as the shelves. And he was wasting precious time; time which he should have employed getting to hell out of it.

The room was stifling. It was hotter than the hot room at a Turkish bath. Round the stove, the embers of a hundred photographs glowed, fanning up into red heat from under the draft from the door, scattering gray ashes over the linoleum. There was a stink of burning. It was as if some monstrous celluloid effigy had been roasted at the stake, leaving only a smell behind.

On the hook behind the door by which Joe had entered a big black photographer's hood was hanging. It must, thought Joe, be very heavy to have pulled the hook half out of the woodwork. He went across, and lifted it. As he did so, his fingers almost touched Herr Hoffracker's face. He was hanging from the hook, which went under the collar of his coat. His face looked quite peaceful. His old head, cocked to one side, had an almost roguish look about it.

He had not died from strangulation. A quick look suggested, rather, that his neck had been broken by a blow from behind.

Joe eased out through the door, turned out the light, and crossed the dim front room. The bell above the street door went ting as he opened it and tang as he shut it. Then he was in the cobbled alley. He hoped that he looked steadier than he felt.

He had seen plenty of dead men before. As a reporter, on roving commission, it had been his job to seek out violent and sensational death. He had seen men shot in riots, stabbed in brawls, burned and crushed in air disasters, and had come to regard them almost as lay figures. He had never before had to consider that the malevolence which had turned on the victims might now—in all probability was now—turned on him.

Ting-tang went a bicycle, shooting past him in the narrow street.

The shop must have been watched. If they had had any doubt about his intentions, this doubt would now be at rest. He was certainly being followed.

But would they *know* that he had gone into the back room? Think. Yes, of course they would. He had turned the lights on before closing the intervening door, and the lights must have been visible from the street. They would guess, therefore, that he had seen the body.

Something hit him in the middle of the back. Three urchins were gaping at him. He picked up their ball and handed it back to them. The children smiled politely at him.

He was at the foot of the hill now. He decided to ignore the tram and walk back to the office. As long as his legs kept moving his mind went on working.

By the time he reached the Adelbodener-Strasse, he was nearly normal again. Better, he had the outlines of a plan in his mind.

There was a crowd in front of the building, almost blocking the doorway. Edging his way past, he saw that two boys were fighting. One had got the other down and was sitting on his chest, pummeling him systematically but without malice. It looked to Joe more like a game than a real fight.

He felt a hand tug at his coat pocket and looked down. It was a small boy with very light, almost white, hair and a marked squint.

The boy grinned at him, squirmed around, and

disappeared into the crowd. He did not look like a pickpocket.

Joe squeezed through the crowd into the hallway. The lift was waiting and empty. He got in and pressed the button for the sixth floor. As soon as the doors were shut, he dipped his hand into his pocket. The boy had not been taking anything out; he had been putting something in. It was an envelope, perhaps four inches by three, sealed with adhesive tape. The enclosure felt like thick paper or thin cardboard.

He ripped it open. It was a photograph, showing the front of the Stadttheater. The figures in the foreground—Humbold, the Bishop, even the microphone he was speaking into—were identifiable, if blurred. But the telescopic lens, by some freak of focus, had picked out the background in clearest detail.

The top of the turret window was open, a few inches, on its ratchet, and through those few inches protruded the barrel of a gun. There was not the slightest doubt about it. You could see the foresight and the fluting of the barrel.

The lift stopped with a jerk. Joe dropped the photograph back into his pocket, slid back the door, and stepped out onto the sixth-floor landing. Then he started very cautiously to descend the staircase. He wanted to make sure that there was not already a reception committee on the fourth floor. He thought it unlikely, but his respect for the opposition was growing.

There was nobody there. Joe found Herr Sand-

holzner at his desk, fixing stamps into an album.
He sat down beside him and told him the whole
story. It was a risk, but the need for an ally was
strong upon him.

Herr Sandholzner listened carefully, and said at
the end, "I should not imagine that the police will
attempt any official action. They would fear the
publicity. Your own newspaper—even our own little organization here—it could hardly be sup-
pressed entirely."

Joe said, "They must know that if this photograph appears in a single foreign paper it blows
them and their schemes sky high."

Herr Sandholzner regarded the photograph
thoughtfully. "There is something very convincing
about it," he agreed. "Possibly they will have seen
the negative themselves. In any event, they will go
to great lengths to get it back."

"What do you imagine they will do?"

"Organize something. A put-up brawl. A knife
in the back. A cord round the neck. A bullet. A
boot."

"Skip the details."

"But, I would guess, *not* before tonight. These
things take time to organize. And they go better in
the dark."

"Then you think I've got until this evening."

"Only if you behave naturally. And make no attempt to escape. If you try to get out, they *must*
move at once."

Joe looked at his watch. He was surprised to see
that it was still only eleven o'clock. A lot seemed to

have happened since he had left his bed that morning.

"Have you got any plan?"

"I have a sort of plan," said Joe. "But I shall need help, and I'm wondering if I ought to involve you."

"They will consider me involved in any case. What had you in mind?"

"You know that place I hired my car from—the little garage behind the Sportplatz."

"Yes."

"Could you go there, as quickly as possible, and hire another car. Any sort of car as long as it's quite different from the one I've got now. With a roof rack and a set of chains for the back wheels if possible. Say it's for a friend of yours who wants an afternoon's skiing."

"I shall have to mention a name. Might I suggest Mauger?" Herr Sandholzner was rummaging in the drawer of his desk as he spoke. "We had here last year a rather objectionable young man of that name. He joined us to report the International Ski Events. Yes. Here they are." He produced a packet of calling cards, neatly embossed: Peter Mauger. Accredited representative of Sportswear, London.

"Fine," said Joe. "See if you can hire skis and sticks and one of those zip-over suits from the big shop on the corner of the platz, and put them in the car too."

"You'll need boots, gloves, thick socks, and some form of cover for your head and ears. It isn't playground skiing on the Dolomiten in winter."

"Buy what you have to," said Joe. "I'll write you an open check on my drawing account. While you're at it, get a small knapsack and put in a bottle of brandy."

"All that I will do," said Herr Sandholzner. "But since this building is undoubtedly under observation, I should be interested to know just how you intend to reach the garage without being followed *and*, what is more important, without appearing to shake off your followers. It will require finesse."

"I had an idea about that," said Joe.

By the time he got out again the street in front of the building was more or less clear. There were a number of men gazing into shop windows, buying newspapers, or talking to other men. Any of them could have been Colonel Julius's police. With the air of a man who has come to a decision, Joe walked to the nearest telephone booth and rang up the British consulate. After a little delay he found himself talking to Evelyn Fiennes.

"Afraid the Consul's out," said Evelyn. "It's the trade adviser speaking. Anything I can do for you?"

"Just to leave a message," said Joe. "I'd like to see the Consul this afternoon or early this evening."

"He ought to be back before lunch."

"Would you ask him if five o'clock will suit him? I'll come round to the consular office. If he can't make it, he can telephone me at the Trans-World Agency."

Evelyn said he was sure this would be all right. Joe thanked him and rang off. Next he went to the big café on the corner of the Maria-Theresien-Strasse, ordered a cup of chocolate, and looked through the morning papers.

The *Lienzer* said that the situation was quiet. The trial of the assassin Boschetto was due to start in two days' time. And there had been further heavy snowfalls, both on the Hohe Tauern in the north and at Oberdrauburg in the south.

Joe looked at his watch. Fifty minutes. He ran over the details of his plan. It depended on the fact that in Lienz, as in all large Austrian towns, there were two police forces. The gentlemen watching him at that moment were from the town police, controlled by Colonel Julius from the Greite-strasse; but there was another force, the gendarmerie, who had a headquarters in the Tiergasse and were responsible for the country districts. Joe, who had a journalist's knack of making useful friends, had already struck up an acquaintance with Rittmeister Kogl, deputy head of the gendarmerie. He and Joe had found a common interest in photography, and Kogl had urged him to spend an hour or two looking over their photographic section. It seemed to Joe that maybe this was the time to take him up on his invitation.

He paid his bill. Ten minutes' leisurely walk brought him to the Tiergasse. He turned in at the main entrance, crossed the forecourt, and opened the plate-glass door. He could not help grinning to himself as he considered the difficulties and complications which this simple move must have created for his watchdogs. It was not that there was any actual hostility between the two forces. In many cases they worked in co-operation. But a member of the town police would think twice about walking into the gendarmerie; and if he did walk in he would almost certainly use the staff, not the public, entrance. In fact, his first and natural reaction would be to get onto his own headquarters for instructions. All of which would take time.

"Rittmeister Kogl," said the sergeant in the front office. "He is, I think, in conference."

"The matter is not urgent," said Joe. "Could you find out for me when the Rittmeister will be free?"

"I will speak to his deputy. Would you kindly wait here for a few moments?"

He held open the door of the waiting room.

As soon as it had closed behind him, Joe whipped out an envelope. It was addressed to the Rittmeister, and contained a note—which he had written while waiting in the café, regretting that he was unable to wait longer on this occasion and hoping to see him shortly. He propped this up in the middle of the table, where it was certain to be seen, went across to the door, and edged it open.

All was quiet. Away to the right he could hear the sergeant speaking into the telephone. He was evidently having some difficulty locating the Rittmeister.

Joe tiptoed down the passage, turned to the right—he was trying to remember the way that Kogl had brought him on his last visit—left at the end, down a shallow flight of steps, and there was the door that led to the parking lot.

No excitement. No shouts. No one at all.

The courtyard gave onto a small service road. People were crossing at the far end, and there was a group of men standing at the corner. Joe turned the other way. For a moment he thought it was a dead end. Then he saw a passage to the left. Once in it, he took to his heels. The passage zigzagged up the hill, then branched into a maze of little side streets. It was the poorest quarter of the town.

When he felt he had put a safe distance between himself and any possible pursuit, he slowed down, took out his street plan, and worked out a route which would bring him to the garage by side streets. This was not difficult. Lienz had developed untidily. It was a warren of small streets, alleys, arcades, and passages, an escaper's paradise.

A quarter of an hour later he presented himself at the garage in the Sportplatz. An elderly Steyr sedan was standing in front of it, with skis strapped to the roof rack. Joe identified himself to the proprietor as Peter Mauger, took possession of the vehicle, and drove sedately out, across the platz, and out of the town.

Half a mile down the road he hit the roadblock. The sergeant in charge examined his skis with professional interest.

"You are English?" he said.

"Irish," said Joe.

"Fine," said the sergeant. "You will find good snow on the lower slopes of the Gölbnerjoch. You take the right turn at Mittewald."

"That's just where I was thinking of going," said Joe untruthfully.

On the main road driving was slow but not too difficult. The plows had cleared a single, wide track. It was half past two when he reached Abfaltersbach. The snow had started to fall again: a few fat flakes, with promise of plenty more to come. Not wanting to block the road, he turned into an open forecourt, got out the chains, and started fixing them onto the back wheels. He had fixed the offside chain and was crouching down behind the car working on the near side one when he heard the noise of engines. Six open troop carriers, each with its contingent of steel-helmeted troops, ground past him and disappeared in the direction of Sillian.

Joe held his breath until the last of them had ground past. Then he finished fixing the second chain. He worked fast. It seemed to him that there mightn't be a lot of time to lose.

Even with chains that side road was almost impassable. First it dropped steeply to the river, then it started climbing and twisting. A track of a sort had been cleared, but Joe realized that if anything was coming down it he was finished. It was not a moment for half measures. He engaged low gear, muttered a prayer, and put the car at the hill. Three nightmare minutes later he was at the top.

He tried to make a quick survey. The trouble was that he dare not stop. Chains or no chains, if he once stopped it was going to be a toss-up if he started again.

The road, as he could see, ran level for some distance, skirting a sharp drop to the right, down to a tributary of the Drava. Away ahead of him a cluster of red roofs marked the village of Kartitsch. He would have liked to get beyond Kartitsch before abandoning the car, but the contours on his map showed the road rising steeply through it. The worst thing of all would be to get stuck in the village street under the eyes of the inhabitants.

To his left, a short way off the road, he saw what he needed: a barn, standing by itself. He swung the wheel round, scudded through the narrow opening, and bumped his way up the track. The big doors of the barn were shut, and padlocked, but he managed to wedge the car between the end wall and a stack of cut wood. It was snowing quite hard now. The tracks he had made would soon be covered.

Joe looked at his watch again. It was half past three. He had two hours of daylight, and he was going to need it all. He put on boots and skis, took a quick nip at the brandy in his haversack, pulled his woolen helmet thankfully over his head, and started out.

The first part was comparatively simple, a rough but uncomplicated ski trek, across the road, down into the little valley, and across the stream, frozen bone hard and hidden under snow.

It was when he started to climb the other side that he realized just how out of condition he was. The reversed skins on the underside of his skis enabled him to get enough grip to keep at an upward angle of perhaps thirty degrees to the line of the slope. This meant plodding uphill in a long zig-zag. In order to keep direction he counted his steps, fifty on a left tack, reverse, fifty on a right tack, reverse.

If the slope had been smooth or the snow had been deeper it would not have been so bad. But two or three times outcrops of rock forced him to make a detour. Soon his breath was coming in gasps and the sweat was trickling down inside his woolen helmet.

After twenty minutes of it he was forced to stop. He was alone in a silent, white, drifting, whirling world. His only guide was the gradient. If he went up far enough he must reach the top. Along the top ran the frontier. Across the frontier was Italy. His mouth was dry. He tried to drink some brandy but it made him feel sick.

In the short time he had been standing, the sweat on his face had started to freeze. It was time to get going again. Fifty left. Fifty right. It was at this point that he struck the track.

Joe blinked the snow out of his eyes and stared. Across his front, at an angle of forty-five degrees, ran a freshly beaten ski track. With the snow fall-ing as it was, it could not have been made more than half an hour ago.

A considerable party of skiers coming down from a mountain hut, he guessed. The broad, firm track they had left would be a help to his weary legs; and he judged, from the direction it was going, that the hut to which it led would be on, or near, the frontier.

Ten minutes later he heard the voices. Then, as a gust of wind blew aside the swirling snow for a moment, he saw above him and to his left the hut, stacked skis in front of it, and a group of soldiers in uniform. It was a mountain patrol he had been following; going up, not down.

Without troubling to turn, he pushed himself backward, down the track. Just as he needed it most, the snow seemed to be thinning. A stronger gust of wind blew it clear. The track turned, and he was out of sight of the hut. He stopped and tried to think.

In an hour it would be dusk. But if he hung about for an hour he would certainly be frozen and might easily be spotted. Now that he was so near, his instincts told him that it was safer to go forward.

The slope above him was too steep for skis, but there was plenty of outcrop, and he thought he might manage it on foot. He unbuckled the skis and laid them carefully along a ledge of rock. Then he started to climb.

Damn it, he had been right. The snow *was* stopping. There followed half an hour of slow scrambling, much of it on hands and knees, in and out of drifts, up exposed ridges of rock, which got steeper as he went up.

Dusk was falling, and Joe was close to the end of his endurance when he reached the spine of the hogback and peered over.

It was an awe-inspiring sight. Away to the left rose the towers of the Hochspitze and the Steinwand, and running down from them the great vertical gash of the Valle Visdende. In front of him the slope fell so steeply that it was almost sheer, to the San Stefano motor road, a streak of jet across the white. Beyond were the lights of Auronzo.

He saw something else too. Twenty yards ahead of him, in the gathering dusk, leaning on his sticks and peering away from him down into the valley, was a uniformed figure on skis.

12

A State of Emergency

BREAKFAST AT THE CONSULATE was not a social meal. Charles ate first, with a copy of one of Trollope's political novels propped up against the toast rack, and he had usually left for the consular offices, three streets away, before Laura put in an appearance.

On this particular morning, he had just poured out his second cup of coffee when he heard the key in the front door; and a moment later Evelyn came in. He was unshaven, and looked as if he had been up all night, which was not surprising, since indeed he had.

"I could do with some of that coffee," he said.

"Frau Rosa's bringing some more. Any news?"

"Lots and lots of news," said Evelyn. "And all of it's bad. In fact, I don't know when I've encountered such a stinking mess before. In the good old days, if Gladstone heard that a diplomat had got shot up in a hostile capital, he'd dispatch a column of all arms to help him out. Now they could skin us alive and boil us in salt water, and all we'd get would be a strong minority protest in the UN. What an epitaph! The Afro-Asian bloc took grave exception. Come to think of it, that would make rather a good last line for a Ballade of Diplomatic Difficulties. Good morning, Frau Rosa. You look remarkably blooming this morning."

"Will you have eggs?"

"I will have eggs."

"I will cook them for you."

"Did you pick up anything definite?"

Evelyn waited until Frau Rosa had gone, and then said, "Yes, I did. And you'd better finish your breakfast before I tell you, because it's not going to improve your appetite."

"Go on."

"The Socialist Radler and Hammerle were tried by a military tribunal last night, on charges of sedition and fomenting resistance to the regime. They were both found guilty."

"They have a right of appeal to Vienna."

"In their case," said Evelyn, "the right is a bit theoretical. They were shot at six o'clock this morning."

"So?" said Charles bleakly.

Unconsciously he had been expecting something of the sort. Not quite as bad. But something like it. The claws were out now. The beast had smelled blood. He would soon be rooting and snuffling for more.

"Something's happened," said Evelyn. "I can't

find out what it is, but it's having the effect of making everyone move faster than they want to. It could be that they have news that the passes are being cleared—a thaw coming—something like that. It doesn't seem very likely."

"Or Humbold may have had a peremptory message from Vienna."

"Messages won't stop him now. He's got the bit between his teeth. And his timetable's fixed. Whatever's happened has had the effect of accelerating it, that's all. Auxiliary troops are moving up toward the frontier. He's got half a dozen standing camps in the mountains just this side of the border. As soon as he's ready he'll have no difficulty in provoking a border incident. Shots will be exchanged with an Italian patrol, the Lienzers will go down the mountainside like an avalanche, and the Tyrol will be reunited. And once it's been done, it's going to be a bloody bold Austrian government that tries to undo it."

Frau Rosa reappeared and said, "I have boiled both eggs to moderate hardness, and have toasted you some bread."

"You understand my tastes to a T, dear girl."

"You desire tea? I had made coffee."

"Coffee will do splendidly."

"I can quite easily make tea. The lady drinks it."

"Don't let's get into a snarl about it," said Evelyn. "Make a pot of each."

Frau Rosa departed. Charles said, "*When* they are ready? Have you any idea what they're waiting for?"

"I think the idea is to dispose of Boschetto first. His trial starts tomorrow. It won't last more than two days—probably only one."

"Forty-eight hours before they move."

"Forty-eight hours before who moves?" asked Laura. She was wearing a dressing gown and looked a bit pale.

"Consols," said Evelyn. "We confidently expect them to go up."

"Stop trying to be funny," said Laura. "I've been listening to you two through the wall. I heard most of it. Boschetto. Troop movements."

"What a shameless girl."

"I think we ought to keep her in the picture," said Charles. "Things really are shaping for a bit of a bust-up. Boschetto goes on trial tomorrow. Once Humbold has disposed of him, he plans to grab the South Tyrol, quick, and sit on it."

"Will he get away with it?"

"It's a sad thing," said Evelyn, "that in this enlightened age a man who is prepared to *do* something—to take some positive action, however outrageous—still has a terrific advantage over people who are only prepared to talk about it."

"Does that mean yes?"

"It means I think he has a fifty-fifty chance."

"One thing sticks out," said Charles. "And that is that you must sit tight. While the trial's on you'll be the most unpopular girl in Lienz."

"Consul's sister torn to pieces by mob," said Evelyn.

"Thank you," said Laura. "I wasn't thinking of going out anyway."

Charles drove to the office. It might have been his imagination but it seemed to him that the streets were emptier than usual.

The consular office occupied three rooms on the first floor of a block in the Tiergartenstrasse, a district of professional offices. The staff consisted of two Lienz girls, one of whom had some pretensions to typing and shorthand, and Gerhardt.

Gerhardt was Charles's clerk. He had friends, relatives, and contacts in every quarter of Lienz and was the source of most of Charles's confidential reports to his superiors.

As he climbed the stairs he was struck by the silence.

His subordinates were usually careful to arrive at least five minutes before he did, to present him with a scene of virtuous activity. Typewriters would be clacking in one room, Gerhardt talking on the telephone in the other. This was the first occasion that he could remember arriving first.

He unlocked the outer door and went in. There was no obvious confusion, but it seemed to him that someone had been through the rooms. Things were not quite in their familiar places. A set of directories which usually stood on the window sill had been shifted onto one of the tables. A filing cabinet had been moved from the wall and put back not quite straight.

Charles went quickly across to the inner room. The big safe in the corner seemed intact. He opened it with his key, and saw, at once, that the safe too had been searched. The codex machine, which he had put back himself, had been shifted, and the personnel file had been taken out and replaced upside down. Since the safe had not been forced, someone else must have a key. This was not surprising. Most foreign powers managed, sooner or later, to equip themselves with keys of their resident diplomats' safes. What was a great deal more serious was the careless way in which the search had been carried out. It suggested that they didn't mind his knowing that his safe had been rifled.

He was considering the implications of this when the telephone rang. It was Colonel Crocker.

"Just thought I'd ring up to see if you were all right," he said.

"Very good of you, Colonel. Has someone been suggesting that I'm ill?"

"Not ill, but I thought you might need a bit of help."

"Help?"

"Friends of mine in the town tipped me off last night. The Hofrat seems to be stirring up some sort of hate against the English."

"I've heard nothing of it."

"Probably all hot air. However, I just wanted to let you know that I had a word with Commander Muspratt and Dr. Grant. We've all got rifles, and we could be at the consulate by car in a matter of ten minutes."

"It's very good of you," said Charles. "I'm sure

the whole thing's a propaganda move of Humbold's."

"The Commander tells me he can probably raise half a dozen more men at the club."

"If anything happens," said Charles, "I'll let you know at once. But I'm quite sure it's a false alarm."

As he rang off he heard footsteps running up the stairs. It was Gerhardt. His brown, wrinkled monkey face was alive with apprehension.

When he saw Charles, some of the anxiety disappeared.

"You are here, Herr Konsul?"

"Certainly." Charles looked pointedly at his watch. "*I* am here."

"My regrets that I am late. I have been round to find out what was wrong with the girls."

"And what was wrong with them?"

"Gertrud has a migraine. Risa has boils."

"I'm sure they'll both be all right in a day or two," he said soothingly. "Suppose we get on with opening the post."

He realized, as he said it, that it was no use. Gerhardt was brimming with news. He was brimming and overflowing with it. It would have been cruelty to impose any further restraint on him.

"My cousin," he said, "who works at police headquarters tells me that an American criminal committed yesterday a murder in the Oberlienz suburb."

"An *American* criminal?"

"He has been masquerading as a newspaperman. He killed a photographer named Hoffracker, in his shop. It is thought that there was a dispute about money. In an endeavor to conceal the crime he set fire to the shop."

"Do you happen to know his name?"

"His name was Keller."

"I see," said Charles. "That's very interesting. Very interesting indeed. I presume he's been arrested."

"No. He escaped the police. He was thought to have been helped by the gendarmerie. There is, as you know, a certain rivalry."

"I knew they were touchy about their rights. I didn't know they helped each other's prisoners escape."

"That part of the story is, at present, obscure."

There were further footsteps coming up the stairs. Not the light steps of Gertrud and Risa; heavy male steps, which came to a clashing halt outside their door.

"Better go and see what they want."

He listened to the sound of the argument: gruff, official voices; Gerhardt protesting, in a voice which rose to a squeak. If something really was going to happen, he wondered whether he would have time to ring up the Colonel.

Gerhardt reappeared and said, "It is Inspector Moll, with some men. He asks you to go with him to government headquarters."

"Asks or orders?"

Gerhardt managed to smile. "It is difficult to say," he said, "but he was most insistent. The message came from Humbold himself."

"I am always at the disposal of the Hofrat," said Charles, collecting his coat and putting on his soft brown hat at the correct Foreign Service angle. He toyed with the idea of taking a rolled umbrella but thought this might be overdoing it.

"When I am gone," he said, "lock the door, and let no one in until I get back. If there is any trouble, you can ring Colonel Crocker, at the English Club, and let him know."

He followed Inspector Moll down the stairs. An armored car was standing in an otherwise deserted street. The inspector gestured politely toward it.

"Thank you," said Charles. "I'll go in my own car."

"My orders—"

"They're *your* orders, Inspector, not mine." He turned about and made for his car. The inspector hesitated, then shrugged his shoulders and climbed into the armored car.

Government headquarters was in turmoil, but it was turmoil backed by some degree of order and purpose. Steel-helmeted motorcyclists were coming and going. A squadron of armored snowcats was parked in the square. The barbed-wire entanglements had been lifted, and command vehicles drawn up on both sides of the entrance were humming with life. When he had visited the building before, it had been a beleaguered fortress. Now it was the headquarters of an army poised for the offensive.

He drove in without trouble and parked his car. Inspector Moll showed him into a small anteroom.

He had only two minutes to wait, when the door opened and Colonel Julius Schatzmann looked in.

His great bulk swaying as he walked, the Gray Bear came across the room and lowered himself in silence into a seat opposite Charles. There was a half-smile on his face, but his black button eyes were as hard as steel and as devoid of meaning.

"Good day, Herr Konsul."

"Good morning," said Charles. "Is it you or your master that I have been brought here under armored escort to talk to?"

"The Hofrat asked for you—"

"Asked is one way of putting it."

"But I am glad you have arrived in good time, since it enables me to have words with you first."

Colonel Julius turned, and the chair creaked under him.

"There are aspects of this matter which are unfortunate. It would have been much better for all of us if your sister had said nothing."

The black eyes waited for comment, but Charles said nothing. His diplomatic training told him that an offer of some sort was in the wind.

Colonel Julius sighed. "I have reached an age," he said, "when all I seek is a quiet life. Nationalistic and racial aspirations are a fine thing—for the young. Between these four walls—and I shall, of course, deny it if you repeat it—but between these four walls, I consider the South Tyrolese are very happy as they are, and I do not think that either side will find a pfennig's worth of advantage in the coming Anschluss."

Charles said, "You speak of it as a certainty."

"Let us say a distinct possibility. But the point of my remarks is this: Where a prize of that magnitude seems to be within reach of a man like my master, he will not be scrupulous in disposing of obstacles."

"No," said Charles, "I imagine not."

"Your sister is an obstacle."

"I fail to see it."

Colonel Julius said, "It is indeed difficult to understand how a charming and intelligent—I mean that—*and* intelligent girl can have allowed herself to get into such a position. But it is undoubtedly true. So many people have now heard her story— so many more people will soon hear it—"

Charles looked up sharply, but the Colonel's face remained bland.

"—that if we fail to call her as a witness at Boschetto's trial, it will be imagined that what she says is true. And it will not be easy to get the verdict we require. For if Boschetto is not found guilty, the spark will be lacking, the people will not march."

"I accept your judgment on the matter," said Charles. "But I fail to see what I can do about it."

The Colonel looked at his watch. "We must go in now," he said. "A proposal will be made to you. I urge you, most strongly, to accept it. It is my official duty to do so. But"—and here he came and sat on the corner of the table, and his voice sank to a soft, rumbling purr—"if you are quite unable to do so, I might be able to suggest an alternative. Come—" He got up and his voice rose to its normal pitch. "We must not keep the Hofrat waiting."

Heinrich Humbold was alone in his office. He did not get up or offer to shake hands. He indicated a chair for Charles to sit in. Colonel Julius remained standing.

"I have to inform you," he said, "that yesterday a very serious thing occurred. An American journalist, Keller, had apparently arranged with a photographer, Hoffracker, to forge a photograph purporting to show a gun being fired from the front of the theater. He seems to have done this in an attempt to support your sister's story. It is suspected that he is an agent of the CIA."

"You have evidence of that?"

"The evidence of it is the unscrupulous way in which he has behaved. He appears to have quarreled with the photographer Hoffracker over the division of the profits, killed him, and burned down his shop to conceal the crime. He then hired a car, drove toward the Italian border, and climbed the mountain track leading to the frontier. There he encountered, and killed, a member of the frontier control."

"I trust," said Charles, "that he was apprehended before he entered Italy."

"Unfortunately, no. Strong representations will be made to the Italian government."

"It would be most improper of them to harbor a murderer," agreed Charles.

"Two of Keller's accomplices have been traced and are under arrest. One is the Lienz representative of the Trans-World Press Agency, Sandholzner. The other is the proprietor of a garage which supplied him with a car. The latter may have been acting innocently. Sandholzner, I am certain, knows more than he has told us—as yet."

Charles said, "I know neither of these men. Nor, in fact, have I ever met Mr. Keller."

"No? He has visited your flat on one occasion at least, and would appear to have been on friendly terms with your sister."

"You may be right. Is it important?"

"It is of considerable significance, in the light of the latest developments. Yes."

Now we're coming to it, thought Charles. He said, in a voice of polite interest, "What developments are those?"

"Yesterday the assassin Boschetto made a full confession."

"Yes?"

"Have no fear, I can assure you that no force of any sort was used. He made this confession quite voluntarily. Indeed, so far as he personally was concerned, any confession was superfluous. There were a thousand witnesses to his crime."

"There were a thousand witnesses to the fact that the Bishop was assassinated," agreed Charles.

Humbold looked at him sharply, and said, "What was more interesting was that he revealed to us something of the background of the crime. It was planned in Italy—to be precise, in Rome. Boschetto himself was selected as a simple-minded patriot, with a grudge. He was got hold of immediately he left prison, was given a gun, and was also given a great deal to drink. His part in the matter was deplorable, but he was only the hand, not the head nor the heart of the killing."

"He must have been a very simple man," said Charles, "to perform, in front of a crowd of witnesses, an act which must inevitably result in his own destruction." And, to himself, as he spotted the gleam of triumph in Humbold's eye, damn it, I believe that's what he wanted me to say.

"Quite so," said Humbold. "The plotters had, of course, considered the point. They had arranged for an accomplice to be present. An accomplice who would distract suspicion from Boschetto by swearing that he was not the killer—that the shooting was done by a mysterious, unknown, untraceable assassin concealed in the theater."

Charles found himself staring at the Hofrat. He opened his mouth, but no sound came.

"Boschetto's confession has made your sister's part in the matter all too clear."

"You cannot be serious."

"Do you know who your sister associated with in Rome?"

"No—but—"

"Did you know that one of her closest friends was Lorenzo Vigari, a notorious Communist intriguer?"

"No."

"It seems that you really know very little about your sister's activities."

Keep your temper, said Charles to himself.

Whatever you do, don't start bellowing. In a voice that he hardly recognized as his own he said, "If you have any proof, any independent proof, of this outrageous allegation, I should like to see it."

"Unfortunately, we have no time for independent proof. Boschetto's trial starts tomorrow. We have, however, prepared a short statement for your sister to sign."

"I can assure you that she will do no such thing."

"There is only one alternative," said Humbold. "Boschetto and your sister, being accomplices, will have to stand trial together."

13

Cousin Franz

"*I* THINK HE'S MAD," said Evelyn.

"Not sure," said Charles. "When a man's playing for high stakes—higher than he can afford to lose—the rules are bound to get a bit elastic."

"Tell me again what he said."

"If Laura would sign this confession, he'd allow her to slip out of the country."

"Did he say how?"

"Yes. He'd got it all arranged. I'd be allowed to drive her as far as Sillian. The road's open now. And the frontier police would have instructions not to stop us. She could be back in Rome by tomorrow night."

"Leaving behind her," said Evelyn, "just about the most frightful diplomatic stink imaginable. There's going to be a big enough row, in all conscience, when young Mr. Keller's story hits the headlines. But when this one breaks, right on top of it: 'Consul's sister aids assassin'—"

"No one will believe it."

"I wouldn't be too sure," said Evelyn. "I don't mean," he added hastily, as he saw Charles's face, "that our masters will believe it. But the rest of the world is pretty credulous about undercover plots. Look at the way the CIA automatically gets blamed for any bother anywhere in the world."

"I shan't allow her to sign it, of course."

"What's going to happen if she doesn't? Were you told that?"

"If she doesn't, they put her on trial with Boschetto."

"Actually on trial? Are they planning to come and drag her out of the consulate?"

"I don't know."

"Because if they do, there really is going to be trouble."

"More than trouble," said Charles. "Bloodshed. A joint services task force, led by Colonel Crocker and Commander Muspratt, is under arms already. They've set up their headquarters in the British Council Cultural Exhibition and they're spoiling for action."

"It looks as if they're going to get it."

"There's one ray of hope. I'm not sure the opposition is quite as unanimous as they'd like us to think."

Charles told Evelyn about his interview with Colonel Shatzmann.

Evelyn said, "You think Julius may have seen the red light? You could be right. It'd be absolutely in keeping with his training and character. He'd back Humbold to the hilt—as long as he was winning. And drop him like a hot brick the moment he thought he'd gone too far."

"I doubt if he's strong enough to stop Humbold doing what he wants."

"Maybe not. But it's useful to know that he's even thinking about it. What's your plan now? Sit tight and stick it out?"

Charles said slowly, "For myself, I'm quite prepared to stick it out. I don't see that they stand to gain anything by antagonizing us. In fact, they'd probably as soon have us on their side. But it's absolutely clear that we've *got* to get Laura out. And on our terms, not theirs."

"Oh, absolutely," said Evelyn. "Have you any idea how? And if we can find a way—something really ingenious, like doing her up as a gross of woolen underwear and dispatching her to Marks and Spencer's—do you think she'll agree?"

"You scout round and find a way out. I'll persuade her to take it."

Charles got back to the flat in time for a late lunch. He found Laura doing a jigsaw puzzle. It was one which his predecessor had left behind. It contained nine hundred and seventy-five pieces and was believed to show a party of kittens tobogganing down a slope. Laura had completed the top right-hand corner.

"There's a bit missing," she said.

"You always think that when you can't do a puzzle."

"I've just counted. There are six kittens and only

five heads. What's the news?"

"Nothing definite. A lot of rumor." He gave her most of the details.

"You don't think I ought to sign this confession. I could always deny it afterwards."

"No," said Charles, "I don't. It isn't only that I'm against signing things that aren't true—and it's very difficult to talk yourself out of a document when you've signed it in the presence of half a dozen witnesses, and probably a television camera into the bargain—and it isn't only that the existence of such a document would cause the biggest diplomatic row since Bernstorff had his portfolio stolen in America in 1916—I've forgotten how I started this sentence."

"You've said 'it isn't only' twice. Then I imagine you were going to say why you *really* didn't want me to sign it."

"You've always had a more orderly mind than I. The real reason against your signing it is that I'm far from certain they'd keep their side of the bargain. Once they'd got your confession they'd think up some reason for keeping you here, and put you on trial too."

"What," said Laura, trying to keep her voice at a nice, steady level, "do you think I ought to do?"

"There's only one answer to that. We've got to get you out of here *without* Humbold's kind help."

"If you did, you'd be in for it, wouldn't you?"

"He'd be very angry with me," said Charles, "but I doubt if he'd actually do anything. There's a prejudice against shooting other people's consuls.

188

And I can't see that it would do him any good. Mind you, Evelyn doesn't agree. He thinks Humbold's mad. If he's mad, he might do anything."

From where Laura stood in the window she could see the street. The apparatus of blockade was now quite open. Wheeled traffic had been diverted at either end of the street and a troop carrier had been backed into position opposite the entrance to the building. An empty ground-floor shop immediately opposite had been taken over as a guard-room.

"Do you think there's any real chance of getting me out?" she said. "I suppose the back way has been blocked now."

"You suppose correctly. There's a guard like this one in the street behind us."

"Then—?"

"Evelyn's out now seeing if he can make any useful contacts. It's no good getting you out of the flat unless we can get you out of the country too."

"I suppose not. Equally, it's no good finding a way out of the country unless you can get me out of the flat."

"I expect we shall think of something. All you've got to do is sit tight and keep calm."

"I am keeping calm."

"You're doing very well," said Charles. "I've got to go round to the British Council Exhibition. If Colonel Crocker shoots anyone, we really shall be in trouble. Don't open the door for anyone except me or Evelyn."

"All right," said Laura. She returned to the puz-

189

zle. The fattest of the kittens was dressed in a flowered muslin smock, not perhaps the most suitable dress for winter sports. It had a smug expression. Laura found its tail and fitted it into place.

After leaving the consulate Evelyn walked down the Maria-Theresien-Strasse, entered a large store by the front entrance, left it immediately by one of its side exits, crossed the road, went into a tobacconist's by its front door, purchased a packet of fifty of those deplorable cigarettes which are known to German students as coffin nails, and left the shop by the back door, which gave onto an alley. This took him into a quiet square, the first of a series that flanked the cathedral.

The last of these squares enclosed a tiny pleasure garden. There was a pond in the middle, and in the center of the pond a bronze nymph. On the top floor of a building overlooking the nymph was the office and apartment of Heinrich Jensen, who described himself as a general agent, a not inaccurate description of the odd, complicated, and curious functions he carried out, and for which he was paid at irregular intervals, in four different currencies. He was tall and very thin, and when he coughed, which he did with perfect regularity every two minutes, he bent himself forward into a hoop.

"So kind of you to bring cigarettes," he said to Evelyn. "They will kill me, of course. This or the next packet, or the packet after."

"You told me that when we first met, ten years ago."

"Did I?" The eyes far sunk in the lined face lit up for a moment. The fire died. "I shall not be saying it in ten years' time. That is for sure. What do you want to know?"

"Anything you can tell me."

"About a prince of the Church and a certain young lady whose eyes were sharper than her discretion."

"About that, yes."

"There is not much to tell you that you will not have guessed already. The shooting was done from the theater, by a youth called Hans Dorf. Boschetto was used as a cover. He had been released from prison the day before. You knew all this."

"What about the gun?"

"Like all professional criminals, Boschetto had a gun concealed. The police knew where it was. One of Boschetto's so-called friends was in their pay. They got it out, fired bullets from it, buried them in the façade of the theater. They planned to make Boschetto very drunk and bring him to the parade. It was a piece of good fortune for them that his brother should have been killed the previous day in the South Tyrol. When he was told that, he really was angry. He would, perhaps, really have shot the Bishop—who can say?"

"What will Humbold do now?"

"Who knows? I am not in his mind."

Evelyn digested this in silence. Outside in the square a child was chasing a pigeon, two dogs were circling each other, and an old woman was clearing snow from the path. It seemed to him outrageous that one man, by his ambition, should have involved the whole of a contented, peace-loving people in blood and strife. Intrigue and violence seemed natural in Algiers or Ankara. They could be stomached in Baghdad or Berlin. But here, in this quiet corner of Austria, they were a foreign importation, a monstrous anomaly.

"I think," said Jensen, "that you will have to take the girl out of the country."

"Easier said than done. Have you any ideas?"

"In the summer it would have been easy. Now I don't know."

"Who is the best man to go to?"

"You are prepared to pay?"

"Yes," said Evelyn. "I think we should be prepared to pay quite a reasonable sum."

"In the old days—before all this trouble was stirred up—the best man to go to would have been Rudolf Engermeyer. He is a South Tyrolese himself. He has a watch and jeweler's business. There were many occasions on which it was not convenient for him to trouble the customs authorities, and he would make the journey on foot. It was thought, too, that he had friends in the Grenzpolizei."

"He sounds just the man."

"I fear that he may have become ideologically involved. He was never a declared member of the Tiroler Boden Bund, but many of his friends were in it. On the other hand, if the sum of money you were prepared to pay was large enough, I think he might forget politics. He would have to be very carefully approached."

"We haven't time to be too careful. Could you ring him up, do you think?"

"If you think it wise."

"It's far from wise, but we've got so little time."

Jensen shook his head sadly. "There is always time to do things properly," he said. He got up and went into his bedroom. Evelyn heard him dialing, heard the murmur of voices, punctuated by Jensen's time-signal cough. The conversation went on for a long time. He moved to the window. The pigeon had flown onto the head of the nymph, the child was chasing one of the dogs, and the old woman had cleared three more yards of path.

Jensen reappeared, and said, "Engermeyer didn't sound very keen, but he said that if you go round in about half an hour he will see what he can do for you."

"It's very good of you."

"I hope it will prove to be good. Do you carry a gun?"

"I've got one somewhere. I don't carry it round with me. Why?"

"I think that for the next few days a gun is likely to be more useful than a clear conscience."

Outside, the red sun was curtsying to the Hochgrabe and the Gölbnerjoch. The sky was mother-of-pearl. In an hour it would be dusk. Evelyn walked slowly through the town. His mind, which should have been devoted to the problems in hand, was running on quite different matters. He was thinking of a villa, which he had rented two years before in the outskirts of Innsbruck and which he had now been told was up for sale. It had a garden, cut out of the side of the hill. And a flat roof on which a couple of wicker chairs could stand, with a table between them, and from which you got a breath-taking view of the mountain peaks running up toward the Brenner.

The address which Jensen had given him was in the suburb of Bad Leopoldsruhe, at the western end of the town. It turned out to be a five-story block of whitestone flats, standing between two other blocks, all built since the end of the war but already beginning to reflect their age and the inferior materials out of which they had been constructed. It was the sort of building, thought Evelyn, in which the central heating constantly broke down, none of the doors fitted properly, and the lift was always getting stuck.

In this last particular he was proved wrong. There was no lift, and Herr Engermeyer, as he discovered from the tablet in the hall, lived on the fourth floor. He climbed eight short, steep flights of stairs and rang the bell. There was no response. He rang again. The bell was working all right. It gave a harsh, purring note, like a cat about to spring. Evelyn bent down, opened the letter flap, and looked through. No light in the hall; no sound.

It was at this moment that he heard footsteps coming up the stairs which he had just climbed. They were coming up cautiously, but quite steadily. There were two, or perhaps three, men walking close together.

In the seconds that followed, Evelyn found time to marvel at his own inefficiency. He had let people know where he was going. He had given them time to prepare for his arrival, and he had come out without a gun.

The footsteps continued to mount.

Evelyn looked again at the door of Engermeyer's flat. It offered no way of escape. Engermeyer, having betrayed him, had either taken himself off or was sitting smugly in the darkness waiting for the executioners to arrive.

Behind him, the stairs led to a fifth story. Evelyn turned, and ran up them. His heavy, English rubber-soled walking shoes made little noise.

There were two doors on the top landing. One led to the roof, and was locked. The other belonged to the flat above Engermeyer. Evelyn bent forward, in the gloom, to read the visiting card pinned to the doorpost. It said "Falwasser." Evelyn pressed the bell. This one had a tinkle, like fairy bells or a cascade of ice going into a long glass.

The steps had reached the landing below and had stopped. A muttered discussion started.

Evelyn came to a quick decision. Herr Falwasser was either out or deaf. Whatever happened, he would be safer inside that front door. He bent down, and pulled off his shoe. There was a square of toughened glass in the door above the latch. He reckoned that if he hit it properly, with the heel of his shoe, he could reach inside and turn the latch.

The noise would bring the opposition running, but he might just have time to get through the door and shut it.

He straightened up, to find the door open and a large, square, gray-haired woman looking down at him.

"Good evening."

"Good evening, Frau Falwasser," said Evelyn in his soft German. "Your cousin Franz sends his kind regards. He told me to be sure and call on you." By this time he had insinuated himself into the front hall. "We must not leave the door open. There are desperate folk about these days." He shut it gently, but firmly. "Let us go into your sitting room, and talk of the old days in Bavaria."

He led the way. After a moment's hesitation, Frau Falwasser followed. She shut the door behind her, and indicated an upright chair, of figured mahogany bolstered with horsehair. Evelyn sat down on it. It would have been a contradiction in terms to call it an easy chair, but it gave him an opportunity to replace his shoe.

"You walk habitually with one shoe off?" inquired Frau Falwasser.

"Not habitually. I detected a stone in it, and was removing it."

"A stone in the shoe can be painful. And how is Cousin Franz?"

"He is in good health, considering all things."

"Considering which things?"

"Considering the bad attack of gout which afflicted him last winter."

"For a man with one leg," said Frau Falwasser, "gout must be a crippling infirmity."

The front doorbell tinkled.

"If I might give you some advice," said Evelyn, "I should *not* open the door. As I came up, I noticed three very doubtful characters hanging about near the entrance. I expect they followed me up."

"What would doubtful characters want with me?"

The doorbell tinkled again.

"They might try to sell you something," said Evelyn. There was a telephone in the corner. If Frau Falwasser made any move to let the men in, he would have to restrain her until help had been summoned. He was glad to note that she made no attempt to get up. It was all very well to talk about restraining her. Frau Falwasser would have boxed in a heavier division than he and looked twice as fit.

"Door-to-door salesmen can be a nuisance," she said. "You must meet my husband."

Evelyn had not heard a sound, but when he turned his head, a small man with a beard was standing immediately behind him.

"Do not trouble to rise," said Herr Falwasser. He limped round, and perched himself on the edge of the table. "You must tell us your name, and all about yourself. And why," he went on, before Evelyn could speak, "you have intruded here, and told us such terrible lies."

"I must apologize."

"Your apologies will be made to the police authorities."

Evelyn was devoting the smaller part of his attention to Frau Falwasser. Most of it was concentrated on the hallway. Had it been his imagination that he had heard footsteps going back down the stairs? There had been no noise outside the door for some minutes now.

"I do not think," he said, "that we should trouble the police too soon. I can explain everything."

"Even Cousin Franz, with gout in one leg."

"I think you had better telephone for the police now," said Frau Falwasser. "And I think that you had better sit quite still while he does so."

Evelyn turned his head and found that his hostess was now holding a small, pearl-handled revolver, which was pointing straight at his stomach.

14

The Schatzmann Gambit

EVELYN WAS CLEAR ABOUT TWO THINGS: that the gun was loaded and that, if he made so much as a move to blow his nose, Frau Falwasser would pull the trigger.

"Certainly telephone for the police," he said. "An excellent idea. If I were to promise not to move from this chair, would you mind pointing your revolver, just for the moment, at the floor? A sudden noise, you understand—anything which startled you—"

"I am not easily startled," said Frau Falwasser. Nevertheless, she lowered her pistol a few inches.

"I detect from his accent," said her husband, "that the gentleman is American. In which case he undoubtedly carries a gun himself, and may surprise you."

"Have no fear," said his wife. "Nothing the gentleman does will surprise *me*."

It took five minutes to summon a police car.

Evelyn was glad to hear himself described on the telephone as a sneak-thief. It was the criminal, not the political, police that he wanted on the scene.

The Feldwebel who came in was not a man who believed in wasting time or words. He listened in silence to Frau Falwasser's story: the thief surprised with his shoe actually raised to break the glass—the devices by which she had enticed him inside—the skill with which she had led him on to give himself away. At the end of it, he said, "In the morning, at police headquarters, at nine o'clock, for a deposition, in writing." Then he jerked his head at Evelyn, and stalked out without waiting for him. The Falwassers looked so deflated that Evelyn was impelled to pat the lady of the house on the shoulders. He said, "Fate moves in a mysterious way her wonders to perform," and left them staring after him.

As he walked toward the police car, he recognized a blond head among the crowd on the pavement. It had already occurred to him that Hans Dorf would probably be on the job. As he went past he blew him a kiss.

At the police station the sergeant in charge started by shouting, but changed gear when he saw Evelyn's diplomatic passport and credentials.

"You have stolen these," he said.

"Actually, no," said Evelyn. "They belong to me. I am the person described. Not a flattering photograph, I admit. Now, do you think we might ring up the British Consul?"

"I regret the telephone is out of order."

"You were using it when I came in," said Evelyn.

"If you would come this way, we shall not detain you unnecessarily."

"You'd better not."

The room he was shown to wasn't a cell, but it had bars on the windows and bolts on the door.

Evelyn sat on his chair, and thought about life. It seemed to get harder and harder. He took a piece of paper and pencil from his pocket, and composed himself to reflection.

There was a flurry of shouted orders in the corridor, a stamping of feet, and a clicking of heels.

"A herd of frenzied Indian elephants," wrote Evelyn.

The door opened, and Colonel Schatzmann came in. He looked at Evelyn in some surprise.

"Are you making your will?" he said.

"I'm writing a poem," said Evelyn. "When the muse visits the poet, she will brook no delay. What rhymes with elephants? Pants, of course:

A herd of frenzied Indian elephants
Has trampled on my colleague's stamp collection
The doyen of the Corps has lost his pants
The Afro-Asian bloc took grave exception.

"You have not lost your sense of humor," said the Colonel. He positioned himself on the chair. It was like a crane driver lowering a motorcar onto a smallish ship. "I have come to discuss with you the highly unfortunate situation which has arisen."

Evelyn studied the Colonel's face, under the strong, unshaded, overhead lighting. As far as the face was capable of expressing emotion, he thought that it showed faint signs of worry. He said, "Unfortunate for whom?"

"For Mr. Hart, and, even more so, for his sister."

"The notorious assassin."

"It is not a matter for joking."

"That's where you're wrong," said Evelyn. "The idea of Miss Hart as an assassin, or the accomplice of an assassin, or anything even remotely connected with assassins, is so ludicrous that even Hofrat Humbold must find it difficult to stop sniggering when he suggests it."

"Young girls do foolish things."

"They don't shoot bishops. Or even help other people shoot them."

"In the present atmosphere, people will believe almost anything."

"Quite so. But how long is the present atmosphere going to last? How long can you keep up the pressure if a court should fail to find Boschetto guilty?"

"There is little doubt about the verdict of the court."

"Little doubt, perhaps. But not no doubt at all. Suppose the court says: 'We've all heard some story about a shot being fired from the theater. We'd like to postpone our verdict until the lady in question has given evidence.' What do you do then? Postpone the invasion of the South Tyrol. You can't keep your chaps hanging about forever on the border. They'll get chilblains."

For a moment, Evelyn wondered if he had gone too far. Then he saw that the lines of worry were still present on Colonel Schatzmann's face. They were, if anything, a little more pronounced. He leaned forward heavily and said, "You are an intelligent man, Captain Fiennes. You make a number of observations to me, some of which I have myself already made to the Landespräsident. But although you state the difficulties with great clarity you do not suggest any solution."

"Have *you* got a solution?"

"Yes," said Colonel Julius, "I have."

"And he had too," said Evelyn to Charles and Laura. "At six o'clock tomorrow morning Laura and I are to leave by the back entrance. My car will be parked round the corner. Colonel Julius says that he can arrange to have his own man actually on guard at that time. But it must be before the guards change. He can't guarantee their successors."

"Why would he do that?" said Charles.

"It's a sort of compromise really. What he wants Laura to do is to slip off quietly without making a confession. In fact, without saying anything to anyone. Then, if anyone refers to her during the trial, the prosecution can say, 'Oh, yes. There was an English lady in the crowd who had some hallucinations about the shot being fired from the theater, but since she has seen fit to leave the country, it really won't be possible to do much about it. In any event, since she has not volunteered to give evidence—has, in fact, run away—we think you can take it that she has thought better of it. Let the trial proceed.'"

"Is it Schatzmann's idea or Humbold's?"

"According to Julius, it's his own idea. He says he's certain Humbold wouldn't agree to it. Humbold wants a full confession, signed, sealed, and delivered."

"Do you believe him?"

"That's a terribly difficult question," said Evelyn. "There are such a lot of unknown factors. For all we know, Vienna may be buzzing with activity. A fall of snow needn't stop a modern army. They may be quite determined to take Humbold by the scruff of the neck and stand no nonsense from him. And Colonel Julius might know this. He controls communications and intelligence. He might *know* that the Tyrol putsch was going to be a flop. And once he knew that, you can bet your last schilling that he'd swap horses. Or, at least, he'd see that he had a spare charger handy."

"And if he helps us, he can say afterwards, 'I wasn't really on Humbold's side at all. Look how I helped Miss Hart.'"

"That's right."

Charles considered the matter. Laura continued obstinately with her jigsaw puzzle. The bottom left-hand corner was all that was undone. There were still two bodies left, but only one head.

"What's your other idea?"

"My other idea," said Evelyn, "is that Colonel Julius is in this, body and soul. All he's planning to do is to get Laura out of the consulate so that she can be picked up trying to escape. Much neater, far easier, saves an international incident."

"And which idea do *you* think is correct?"

"I think the Colonel's playing this one straight. Straight with us, that is, and crooked with Humbold. He's been backing both sides of the board, and laying off his bets, for so long that it's second nature to him."

Charles sighed. "It's Laura who's taking the main risk. She ought to have some say in this."

"Of course," said Laura. "*What* a swindle. One of the kittens has fallen off the toboggan. You can only see his body. It's upside down, and his head's buried in the snow."

"Have you been listening to anything we've been saying?"

"More or less," said Laura. "I'm willing to try it if Evelyn is."

At ten to six the next morning, Laura tiptoed through the dentist's waiting room. She was warmly dressed, in windbreaker and trousers, with one of Charles's sweaters underneath, but she was aware of a cold feeling in the pit of her stomach.

She had said good-bye to Charles and had been kissed by a tearful Frau Rosa. It had been difficult to tear herself away from the corner of England represented by the consular flat.

Evelyn went ahead of her. He had breakfasted off whisky, had omitted to shave, and was in a vile temper.

The kitchen door of the restaurant was ajar and a sleepy cook ignored them pointedly. They went through into the foyer of the restaurant. Evelyn thumbed down the latch, glanced at his wrist watch, and edged the door open.

An army truck was parked on the other side of the street, its back to the restaurant, its hood partly closed. A wooden-faced, middle-aged reservist, with a machine pistol over one shoulder, was sitting on the step of the truck, looking at nothing in particular.

"I hope he's our man," whispered Evelyn. He opened the front door, and stepped out. Laura followed. The reservist continued to look at nothing.

They stepped delicately along the swept paving, their feet crunching in the thin blanket of snow that had fallen overnight. When she reached the corner Laura found she had been holding her breath, and let it out with a sigh.

The car was backed down an alleyway at the end of the street. Evelyn unlocked it, climbed in, and pressed the starter. The motor ground round three or four times, reluctantly, once very slowly, and then stopped. Evelyn collected the starting handle off the back seat, got out, kicked the car, and started to crank. After a few moments the engine roared into triumphant life.

As they nosed up to the mouth of the alleyway, another car crossed them, going fast. Laura caught sight of the man sitting beside the driver, and for a split second his eye caught hers.

They swung right, with a jolt which threw her against the door, and left into the Kirchstrasse. As the car gathered speed, she said, "Did you see who was in that car? It was Dorf, and I'm pretty certain he saw me."

"I'm quite certain he did," said Evelyn. "And did you see who was driving?"

"No. I was looking at Dorf."

"It was an old friend of yours, handsome Helmut the he-man."

"If they saw us they'll warn the police posts."

"Maybe," said Evelyn. "But it mayn't do them a lot of good. The post on the Oberdrauburg road has been fixed for us too. I should be more inclined to think they'd come straight after us. Helmut fancies himself—" the car screamed in protest as Evelyn twisted it round a sharp corner—"as a driver, doesn't he?"

"I believe he does," said Laura, jerkily.

"Don't worry," said Evelyn. "It's only good drivers who have crashes. I'm far too bad to come to any harm. This looks like the post ahead."

The road was blocked by overlapping barricades of wood and barbed wire. Two soldiers, one wearing a corporal's stripes, were warming their hands at a brazier, and an armored car was parked on the verge, its twin machine guns pointing absentmindedly skyward.

Evelyn cranked down the window, leaned out, and spoke in German to the corporal. Laura heard the name "Schatzmann" repeated more than once. The corporal peered at the number plate, crossed the road, and disappeared into the house.

"What's up?" said Laura.

"He thinks it's all right," said Evelyn, "but he wants a bit of support from authority. I hope he doesn't take too long."

"Will Helmut know we've gone this way?"

"He'll try the Sillian road first. That's the obvious exit. When he doesn't find us there he'll know it's this or Obervellach. Come on, come on."

A sergeant appeared. He had a paper in one hand. He barked at the soldier, who jumped to the barricade and pulled it aside. The corporal lent a hand. The sergeant saluted. Evelyn returned his salute. Then he pressed the self-starter, which on this occasion did its stuff.

They bucketed off down the road.

"It's about fifteen miles to Oberdrauburg," said Evelyn. "Luckily no one could go very fast on this stretch."

He was descending a steep, twisting section of road at what seemed to Laura to be criminal speed.

"Is it like this all the way?" she managed to say.

"More or less. The road keeps to the left bank of the river."

"Just so long as *we* keep to the road."

208

"What did you say?"

"Nothing," said Laura. They slid down the hill, cornered, and went into a grinding ascent, wheels spinning.

"Like going up a moving staircase coming down," said Evelyn. He sounded a mite more cheerful, and Laura was emboldened to ask, "What happens when we get to Oberdrauburg?"

"We go through it—if they let us. And out of it on the road to Mauthen. I doubt if we shall get that far. We certainly shan't get any farther."

"Why not?"

"Because the Plöcken Pass has been blocked for weeks. It's only a summer pass, really. We leave the car in Mauthen and find a man called Rudi. He takes us over into Italy. What's wrong now?"

"Did you hear that?"

"I can't hear anything except this damned car."

"There's another car behind us."

"It's a public road."

"I'm pretty certain it's Helmut's car."

"Damn and blast," said Evelyn. "Are you sure?"

"Pretty sure, yes. Yes, it is. He *is* coming fast, too."

"If I had a car like his, instead of this old car, I could drive fast," said Evelyn.

As he spoke, they were grinding slowly up a long, left-curving slope bitten into the side of the hill. Above them was partly cleared woodland. Logging had been going on. Ahead the road leveled, and then turned abruptly into the descent.

"Do you think we could get the car up a path

into the forest and let them pass?"

"Not a chance. They'd spot our tracks."

"They'll catch us on the next uphill."

"Like hell they will," said Evelyn.

He stamped on the brake pedal. The car skidded violently, fortunately to the left, rammed the bank, and came to a standstill on the short stretch of level road. They had rounded the curve and were, for a moment, out of sight of the pursuit.

Evelyn was out before the car had stopped. He ran to the roadside and started hurling logs which were stacked there back down the road.

As the other car came round the corner, he heaved up a large billet, and tossed it, like a caber. Helmut was a better driver than Evelyn, and that was his undoing. For he managed to brake without skidding, but his car was still on the steep, ice-crusted slope. Evelyn picked up a smaller log, and threw it. It bounced off the bonnet, and starred the windscreen. Even before it landed, the car was sliding backward, its wheels locked, its speed increasing. Steering and brakes were both equally valueless. It was on a toboggan run.

Fascinated, Laura watched its backward progress. Helmut had released the brakes, which was the correct technique, but as the wheels stopped sliding and started to revolve, so the speed increased.

Halfway down there was a turn in the road. Laura had just time to think, If he can negotiate that he'll run safely back to the bottom again.

But he was going much too fast. The rear near-side wheel of the car hit and uprooted one of the kilometer stones. Then it tried to climb the bank, crabwise, rolled onto its side, wheels spinning, completed the roll, and went down the steep bank beyond in a succession of heart-stopping crunches.

15

Evelyn Comes Clean

"You'd better stay right here," said Evelyn.

Laura, who had her eyes tight shut, nodded. Evelyn was away for about ten minutes. When he came back he found her sitting on the log pile.

"Are they both dead?"

"Yes," said Evelyn. "Quite dead."

"I don't care about Dorf. I'm sorry about Helmut."

"We've got better things to do than being sorry. First there's all this wood to pick up. Try to put it back exactly as it was stacked."

"Why?"

"It may have escaped your attention," said Evelyn, who seemed to be in an evil temper, "that we have just written off the ruler's right-hand man, and the right-hand man's number one boy. And we're not out of the jurisdiction yet. If you want to be charged with a double murder, I don't."

They replaced the logs carefully, shoveled some snow down on top of them, and stamped out the more obvious marks in the road.

"Now," said Evelyn. "I wonder if we can arrange something that looks as if it might have been natural."

After some thought he selected an overhanging boulder, jutting from the bank. Using the jack handle and a stick, they loosened it and let it roll down into the road.

"Won't that mean the next car'll do the same thing?" said Laura.

"I don't think so," said Evelyn. "It was only because Helmut was so bloody clever that he managed to stop at all. Any ordinary driver will run straight into it. Now get in. We've got quite a way to go."

The next kilometer stone said "Oberdrauburg— 8."

"What are we going to do when we get to Oberdrauburg?"

"We aren't going there. Daren't risk it. They'll almost certainly have telephoned ahead. We'll park the car this side of the town and walk round it. It'll be a bit farther, but much safer. Have a look at the map while I drive."

"It looks," said Laura, trying to steady the map, "as if there's a turning-off to the right. It goes through a place called Flaschberg. Then back to the main road the other side of Oberdrauburg. If you wouldn't drive quite so fast I might—yes—

that's it. Stop! Stop! Here's where we turn off."

"No need to shout," said Evelyn.

They went down a track between steep earth banks, crossed the bed of a river, and bumped through the long village street of Flaschberg, without attracting more than the wide-eyed stares of children. From there the track climbed back to a junction with the main road.

The gradient at this point was the steepest they had hit. The old car grumbled and shook in its lowest gear. Evelyn alternated encouragement and abuse as if it had been a tired horse. At the top of the climb they stopped.

"Loosen the girths and give her a breather," said Evelyn. He got out and patted the bonnet. Laura climbed out and stood beside him. Her legs were trembling.

Ahead of them the road curled down, hugging the contours of the hill, to a point where the onion-shaped church spire of Kötschach showed above the trees. Beyond that the road rose again, even more steeply, then started to twist and turn in a series of breath-taking hairpin bends as it climbed to the skyline.

"Is that Italy?"

"The frontier runs along the top of that ridge. You can see the roof of the frontier control post. It's got a flagstaff on it. That's the Plöcken Pass."

"How far?"

"Six or seven miles as the crow flies. If we were a pair of crows we could be in Italy in about half an hour. An inspiring thought."

"What do we do now?"

"We park the car, and walk, keeping off the road as much as we can. We're making for Mauthen. You can't see it from here, it's under the bulge of the hill. That's where we pick up Rudi."

"Where are we going to leave the car?"

"You ask such a lot of questions," said Evelyn. "How the devil should I know where I'm going to leave the car? I've never been here before in my life. You've got the map."

"There is a tiny place marked halfway down the hill. It's called Lass."

"Fine. We'll try that."

Lass was bigger than it looked on the map: a main street, a church, further houses up the hill behind it, and a gasthaus.

"Just what the doctor ordered," said Evelyn. He drove the car into the forecourt of the gasthaus and parked it. "Remember, we're botanists. We're parking our car here while we continue our searches for a particularly rare species of edelweiss."

"In this snow?"

"Certainly. Edelweiss grows only in the snow."

The landlord, a youngish, freckle-faced man, served them with coffee. He was quite agreeable to the car's being left in his courtyard. When he heard that they planned to walk, he looked serious, and said something in German too rapid for Laura to follow.

"What's he getting so worried about?"

"The Plöchen has a bad reputation. It's an old smuggler's route. A lot of bad characters around,

215

according to our host. He wanted to know if I was armed."

"What did you say?"

"I told him that I had no armor but my own impregnable virtue. It's not true, actually. I've got a gun. I sincerely hope I don't have to use it."

"Why?"

"Because I'm a very bad shot. The last time I fired it, I hit myself in the foot. Hurry up and finish your coffee. We ought to get moving. *Now*, where's our landlord got to?"

They stood in the dark hall, which smelled of pinewood and caraway seeds.

There was a faint murmur of conversation from the farther end. Evelyn tiptoed to the door marked "Küche," turned the handle gently, and opened it. Then he closed it, equally gently, and came back.

"I think we'll get out of here. I'll leave some money. I should think five schillings would be enough for a couple of coffees, wouldn't you?"

"What's up?"

"There's no reason why our landlord shouldn't be telephoning the gendarmerie at Mauthen," said Evelyn, as they set off down the road. "He might be applying for a new dog license. I think, though, that the sooner we get off the highway the better. And I think we'll give Mauthen a miss too. Rudi's farm is said to be west of the frontier road, and about five kilometers up it. We should be all right if the snow isn't too deep."

"What happens if it is too deep?"

"You have a remarkable flair for asking unan-

216

swerable questions," said Evelyn. "Presumably we shall sink into it, and stay there in a state of suspended animation until next spring. When the snow melts, they will find us clasped in each other's arms."

"I can hardly wait."

It was all right when they were on the move. It was only when they were standing still that she felt shivery.

It took them half an hour to slither down to the little crossroad. (It was, had she known it, the continuation of the same road on which, nearly forty twisting miles to the west, and two days earlier, Joe had abandoned his car.) It was deep in snow. No wheels had passed along it since the last fall.

Ahead of them rose the twin peaks of the Mauthner Alpe and the Mooskofel.

"Do you mean to say," said Laura, "that we've got to climb *that*?"

"Certainly not. We're going to make our way up one of the side valleys. We want to strike the frontier road just before it starts to hairpin."

It may not have been real climbing, but it was the hardest work Laura had ever set herself to. The gradient was killing; and since the steepest ridges were the ones with the least snow on them, it was these that Evelyn selected. He stopped from time to time to consult a compass which he had strapped to his wrists, but these were the only halts.

First they worked their way up an endless, whalebacked ridge. From the end of this they scrambled, diagonally, across and up, onto a second ridge, flatter than the first and crowned with a fringe of stunted pine trees.

For some minutes past, Evelyn had been looking anxiously over his shoulder. Now he stopped to listen. The blood was pounding so hard in Laura's head that she could hear nothing. Abruptly he seized her, dragged her down into a hollow between the roots of the pine trees, and fell on top of her.

"What is it?"

"Keep still."

A shadow crossed the snow. She saw it and heard it at the same moment: a helicopter, flying not more than a hundred feet up.

"Did they see us?"

"I don't know. I don't think so. Thank God for the trees. If we'd been in the open, they couldn't have missed us. We've got to hurry."

"I can't go any faster. Really, Evelyn, I can't."

"We've got to get under cover before that flying mousetrap gets back. It's all downhill now."

"I can't do it."

"Come *on*."

He had her by the hand, and, incredibly, they were running; running, jumping, and sliding. They were in a sunken track with high stone walls. At the end was a gate. On the gate a young man with apple-red cheeks and light, almost white, crew-cut hair stared at them in astonishment. Evelyn said something, in the gruff, Tyrolese argot, and a slow smile spread across the boy's face. He opened the gate for them. Laura staggered through. Her knees felt as if they were coming un-screwed at the hinges.

They crossed the stone-flagged court and knocked at the door. A woman opened it. Evelyn did some more talking, and they went in. The ground floor of the house seemed to be one big kitchen, dark but blessedly warm. She found her-self sitting on a wooden settle by the fire.

The conversation went on. First the woman, then Evelyn, then the woman again. The skin on either side of her forehead felt as if it had been drawn too tight, her mouth was dry, and there were areas of her body which did not belong to her.

Evelyn came across.

"Rudi's out," he said. "He'll be back in about an hour. His wife wants to know if we'd like some-thing to eat."

"If I try to eat anything I shall be sick."

Evelyn looked at her and said, "What you want is bed. Three or four hours' sleep."

"I'd rather sleep than eat."

Evelyn spoke again to the lady, who nodded sympathetically and beckoned to Laura to follow her.

They climbed a steep, ladderlike staircase and emerged in an attic, clean and white and light. The bed was a boxlike affair under the window.

Laura took off her windbreaker and skiing trousers, climbed onto the bed, and pulled the blankets over her. In a little while she began to feel warmer.

Although she lay there for four hours, unconscious of time, she never really slept. A quarter of her mind was awake. Her body was climbing hills, which got steeper and steeper. Always ahead was a skyline. It was illuminated along the edge, in a curious way, as if, beyond it but out of sight, bright lights were blazing. On her side there were gullies, deep in shadow, leading to the crest. It seemed important to choose the right one. If she chose the right one, it would lead her to the top, to the lights, and to freedom. If she chose the wrong one, something unpleasant was going to happen. As she cowered in the snow, a shadow wheeled over her and something touched her.

She cried out, and sat up. Evelyn was standing beside the bed.

"Sorry to disturb you," he said. "Rudi's back. We ought to start thinking about the next lap. How are you feeling?"

"Better," said Laura. "I've sweated pints."

She still felt weak, but her head was much clearer.

"Do you think you could eat? You ought to have something, if you can. Soup and bread. Or a glass of wine."

This made Laura laugh.

"What's up?" said Evelyn suspiciously.

"It's you," said Laura. "First you drag me up a mountainside, like the monstrous bully you are. Then you sit on the end of my bed, like an old family doctor, prescribing chicken broth and a glass of red wine."

"I'm a man of many parts."

"You'll be feeling my pulse next."

Evelyn went to the door, said something to the lady of the house, and came back.

"A late luncheon—or, in the alternative, an early supper will be up in five minutes," he said. "There's plenty of time. You can't leave before dusk. And that's not until about seven o'clock at this altitude."

"Are you coming with me?"

"As far as the frontier."

"Then what?"

"Then I shall go back and hold your brother's hand."

Laura propped herself up on one arm and said, "Do you enjoy your job, Evelyn?"

"Not very much."

"Then why do you do it?"

"It's that or starve."

"Be serious."

"I am being serious," said Evelyn. "Intelligence work is the only job I'm trained for. It was my father's fault. He was crazy about languages. You know how fathers work out their own ambitions through their sons. Train them from birth to swim the Channel or play cricket for England. Well, my old man was determined that I should be the linguist of the century. We started with German, of course, because it was the twenties, and everyone had their eyes on the next war already. I was brought up in Germany. Went to a German school, and did sums in pfennigs and marks, and learnt how Blücher had won the battle of Waterloo. But that wasn't enough for my father. We spent our holidays in France and Spain, and we had a Spanish cook. Then, when I was about ten, and spoke German and French and Spanish like anything, he got a bee in his bonnet about Russia. So we added a Russian gardener to the ménage."

"It sounds fun."

"It was damned hard work. How would you like doing German all day, Russian in the evenings, and French and Spanish in the holidays?"

"I'd rather do it than Latin and hockey. What happened then?"

"What happened next was the war. No ordinary soldiering for me. Not on your life. Special service. In the course of six years I think I was in every damned silly outfit in the army. I didn't volunteer for them. I was drafted. I was dropped out of airplanes, landed from submarines, went for long, circular tours in the desert, was smuggled across frontiers. There was even a project, I remember, of lowering me from a helicopter."

"That sounds like fun, too."

Evelyn said, quite seriously, "You're quite wrong. It might have been fun to start with. But the novelty wore off. I got to loathe every moment of it. I was never very brave, and any courage I started with had evaporated long before the war was over."

"Courage can't evaporate."

"I'm telling you the truth, the whole truth, and

"For God's sake," said the woman, "take her and go."

Evelyn kissed her quickly on the nose, and she followed Rudi out through the back of the kitchen and into a smaller courtyard behind; then over a cow wall and up a track which rose and twisted.

Left to himself, Evelyn stood for a moment in the dimness of the kitchen. The lady of the house had disappeared. The roar of the engines grew louder.

Moving with great deliberation, Evelyn shut and bolted the kitchen door and mounted the ladder that led up to the sleeping quarters.

The window behind the bed gave a view of the yard. As he opened it the nose of an armored half-track appeared around the corner; a man in the gray uniform of the auxiliary police jumped down from beside the driver and started to fumble with the catch of the gate.

Evelyn, with a look of extreme distaste, extracted an automatic pistol from the inside pocket of his coat, took careful aim, and pulled the trigger. The bullet struck the cupola of the armored car and ricocheted off it with a metallic screech.

The man at the gate stopped what he was doing and dived behind the wall. The machine gun mounted in the cupola swung ponderously round, there was an angry chattering noise, and the top part of the bedroom window disintegrated into a mess of flying glass and splintered wood.

But Evelyn was already out of the room. He had crawled along the passage to the window and was taking a careful look. The man who had dismounted chose this moment to poke his head around the wall. Evelyn fired once more, hitting the track of the vehicle. Although the shot had gone nowhere near him, the man took the hint and disappeared rapidly.

Evelyn looked at his watch. He had no intention of dying a hero's death or, indeed, any other sort of death as long as the event could be postponed. Laura had already had ten minutes' start. Another five minutes, and she should be absolutely safe.

Further time went by. The silence continued unbroken. Then he heard the engine of the armored car start up. He decided that it was going to come straight through the gate. There was the noise of the engine accelerating. He risked a quick look. The car was not advancing, it was retiring.

Other things were happening too.

The lane outside the farm seemed to be full of men. They were certainly not auxiliary police. Their uniform was olive green, not gray, and they were wearing baggy overalls and curious, close-fitting helmets.

Evelyn went back into the bedroom, hid the pistol carefully on top of the wardrobe, and went downstairs. As he reached the kitchen, someone was hammering on the door.

He opened it, and an officer came through. He carried no visible weapon, and the two men who walked behind had their machine pistols slung round their shoulders. Behind them he could see that the yard was already full of men.

Evelyn saw the wings embroidered on the officer's overalls, and comprehension dawned.

"Parachute troop," he said.

"Twelfth Regiment, Second Airborne Division from Vienna," said the officer. "Major Amsbacher."

"Captain Fiennes," said Evelyn. "And am I glad to see you!"

Major Amsbacher said, "Perhaps you could explain what is going on. I heard firing."

Evelyn did his best.

At the end the Major said, "Much of this is outside the scope of my immediate mission. The First Division has already taken control at Lienz. Our orders are to disarm certain irregular camps which have been formed in the frontier area. We do not anticipate any trouble."

Evelyn looked at the men who were standing in the courtyard. They had the reassuringly casual look of regular troops.

"I'm sure you won't have any trouble at all," he said. "I wonder if you could spare a few men to go after Miss Hart."

The Major's eyes lit up.

"Miss Hart," he said. "That is the lady all the newspapers are speaking of. The Consul's sister. Yes?"

"That's the one," said Evelyn. "I didn't realize she'd got into the papers, though."

"In all the papers. It will be a pleasure to help."

"You'll have to hurry. She's had nearly half an hour's start, and she's got the best guide in the Tyrol."

16

Exit of a Heroine

RUDI LED OFF AT A DECEPTIVE, shuffling pace which looked slow but was too fast for Laura. After he had been forced to wait for her once or twice, he slowed it down a little.

When she heard the machine gun open up, she hesitated. Rudi grunted out something in his incomprehensible argot. She gathered that he was saying that they would not be caught now.

The track they were following climbed steadily along the south side of a long, shallow valley, twisting among smooth, rounded rocks scattered haphazard, as if a giant had been playing at bowls. Since the setting sun was in her eyes she knew that they were going due west.

It took them an hour to reach the end of the valley and to climb out of it. Beyond the crest lay an upland plateau, rounded like a shallow saucer, tilted gently upward toward the immediate skyline. In the center of the saucer was a small lake. In summer it must have been an enchanting place, a private paradise of close-cropped grass, mountain flowers, and blue water. Now, under its mantle of ice and snow, with the red sun of a winter's evening going down behind the mountains, it had a desolate look.

Ahead of them a rising wind was blowing puffs of sugar-icing snow off the crest.

Rudi had increased his pace. She thought he was beginning to look anxious and drove herself to keep up with him.

They skirted the lake, passing a derelict wooden hut at its head. Rudi pointed to it and said something. She could not understand his words, but she could understand the look in his eyes. He was frightened.

"Guards?" she said. "Soldiers?"

Rudi shook his head violently, and pointed again.

She looked more closely at the hut. It had been set on stout log piles, above the head of the lake, at a point where a little stream ran down the throat of the valley, and it was evidently designed as a shelter for summer hikers and picnickers. It consisted of a single room, with a veranda in front. The windows were now shuttered, and the double door at the back of the veranda was padlocked.

"What is it, Rudi?"

He pointed to the ground in front of the steps leading up to the veranda. There were footmarks in the snow.

Someone had come up to the hut and had spent

some time walking around it, possibly trying to break in. On the ground beside the steps there was an empty cigarette packet, of the cheapest Austrian brand, and what looked like a piece of very stale bread.

It looked innocent enough. Then she noticed something that did puzzle her. It was the footprints. They had been made by partly naked feet.

There was one clear print in the snow, underneath the shuttered window. The man who had made it had been wearing either a very old shoe or some sort of sandal. The marks of all five toes were very clear in the snow.

Rudi was tugging at her sleeve.

"How far?" she said.

He showed her five fingers, and then another three.

Eight of something? Eight hundred meters, she guessed. About half a mile. She smiled at him reassuringly. Having come so far, she wasn't going to fail at the last fence.

The path they were following led out of the top of the valley. The sinking sun had swung across to their right side. They were going south now.

The path became steeper. They were in a small, but steep, ravine. It was exactly what Laura, in her youth, had supposed the Khyber Pass would be like, a knife gash in the crest of a mountain range, narrow, dangerous. On the one hand, a place for ambush; on the other, the gateway to freedom and safety.

Rudi, who was a few paces ahead of her,

stopped suddenly. He was listening. In that high place the silence was absolute.

Rudi turned his head. He was suspicious, for no reason that she could see, of a mass of rock which overhung the path to the right, and formed an elbow in the ravine. He took a few cautious steps toward it.

At that moment a portion of the rock seemed to detach itself. Laura glimpsed huge arms upraised, saw a bearded face and an open mouth. Then an enormous boulder hit Rudi full in the chest, throwing him onto his back and leaving him flat in the snow, arms and legs spread-eagled.

The shock was so extreme that it drove the breath out of her like a fist in the stomach. Then, as she half turned in her tracks, someone was bounding down the slope toward her, capering grotesquely as he came.

It was an enormous man. Her first impression was simply of size. When he reached the path he stooped and grinned at what was left of Rudi, then executed a little jig. He was as pleased as if he had brought down a difficult bird, on the wing, with one snap shot.

As he straightened up and came toward her, he seemed, to her hypnotized senses, to be bowing from the waist, like a dancer in a ritual marriage dance emerging from the corner to claim his bride.

The face was hidden under a forest growth of matted hair and tangled beard out of which two tiny black eyes glittered jovially. The body was decked in the rags of other men's clothes, botched together with sacking and string. Bare toes stuck out from the wreck of canvas shoes.

He was half a dozen paces from her when Laura wrenched herself round and started to run. She was aware of the pad of feet pumping after her, once, twice, and then, as she stumbled, something heavy, but curiously soft, descended on her head, and she fell forward into blackness.

She was in church.

It was dim, and she felt sick, as she often did when she went with her mother to early service without eating. Also someone was chanting.

Consciousness came back slowly, and in waves.

She was lying on some sort of pallet on the sloping floor of a cave. It was not a very thick pallet. She could feel the stones through it.

The cavern was not more than three feet high, but rough attempts had been made to render it habitable. Two or three planks had been wedged in to block the end of it, and from nails in the planks hung an old coat, a couple of traps, and a dead mountain hare, tied by its feet.

This put her in mind of something, and she looked down to find that her own feet had been hobbled. Apart from this she did not seem to have been harmed.

She turned her head, and the stabbing pain brought tears to her eyes and blinded her for a moment. As the tears cleared, she saw the rest of her habitation. It was very simple.

To the right, and almost within reach, lay the top of a table, without its legs. On it stood a saucer of oil, with a lighted wick floating in it. There were other things on the table: a tin plate, a table knife, the blade of which, she could see, had been whittled almost away with sharpening; a half loaf of bread, and a very large, old-fashioned revolver.

All this time the singing continued. It was a quavering chant, breaking from octave to octave, and it came from outside the mouth of the cave, where the man was squatting. She could make out his bulk, which blocked the low opening. She wondered what, exactly, he was doing, sitting outside in the freezing cold serenading the setting sun. As her other senses returned, she realized other things too. It was bitterly cold inside the cave; cold, and foul-smelling; carrion and filth, the smell of an old man-eater's lair.

Her stomach revolted, and she turned on her side and was miserably sick.

Somehow this cleared her wits. Her feet were lashed together, but not fastened to anything. Her hands were free. She had a limited radius of movement. And there was a revolver on the table. She realized—and for a moment was startled by the realization—that she would have no compunction about using it. Her prayer was that it might be loaded.

She edged across, until her fingers touched it. As far as she could tell, she made no sort of sound. But the man outside the cave had hearing like a wild beast's. The singing stopped, and he half turned.

There was a moment of paralysis. Then she

grabbed at the gun, and he had turned and was coming for her. Her awkward fingers stumbled onto the trigger, and she pulled it.

Nothing happened. Nothing at all.

Either the gun was empty or the safety catch was on. She had no time to find out. She was sprawled, on her side, half on the pallet, half on the floor when he landed on top of her, the impact of his arrival rolling her right over onto her back.

Her right arm was flung wildly out, and her knuckles hit the tabletop with a crack, the useless revolver flying out of her fingers.

Then he was on top of her, pinning her to the ground, exactly as the boulder had pinned poor Rudi. His face was almost touching hers, and she could see his little black eyes, shuttling backward and forward as if they were looking, wildly, furiously, for something that they knew was there, something which had been so cunningly hidden that they could not find it.

The weight was lifted from her as he raised himself on his left elbow. A hand, black and in-grained with dirt like a dog's pad, reached out, caught the front of her windbreaker, and tore it open.

At that moment her right hand closed on something cold. It was the handle of the table knife. She picked it up. No hurry. Plenty of time. She drove it in, once; and then, as the man on top of her arched upward, again and again and again.

He was back on top of her, but now he felt quite different. He was a dead weight. The black eyes were open, but they had stopped flickering and shifting. They had a look of serenity, as if their owner had, at long last, found what he had been seeking.

Blood was dripping, warm, onto her bare skin. It seemed to take her hours to get out from underneath his weight. Further hours to saw through the rope round her ankles. Then she was at the door of the cave, crouching and looking out.

It was still light enough for her to see the path. It lay directly below her. She started to slither down toward it, catching her foot and wrenching her ankle, and crying out; but going on.

Then she was on the path, going forward at a stumbling run. She passed Rudi, stepping over his outstretched legs with scarcely a glance. Her full meal of horrors had left her no room for the least morsel more.

Ahead of her the last, red light of the dying sun slanted along the crest, marking it as sharply as if it had been the end of the world.

Then she was looking down, into a great pit of luminous darkness. Below her, far, far below her, lights were winking, the friendly lights of Italy. She knew that she could never get there. They were as distant as the stars.

It was the cold that drove her on; the cold, and the instinctive feeling that if she stopped moving she would be finished.

Time lost its meaning. She remembered falling twice, and on the second occasion finding it difficult to get up; she remained on her knees, the tears rolling down her cheeks. Then, placing the palms of her hands on the snow and forcing herself to her feet, she staggered on once more.

It was after this, but how long after it she had no idea, that a small, dark figure seemed to rise from the ground in front of her, and a sharp voice said "Dove andate? Da dove venite?" After that things became confused. There were voices, and there were lights, bright lights, which hurt her eyes, but soft voices which spoke the Italian she understood.

Then she was in a different place. Two soldiers in green uniform were holding her under the arms, supporting her. They lowered her into a chair, beside a table. On the other side of the table sat a stout major. She recognized the uniform he was wearing. Lorenz had once pointed it out to her. She was pleased with her cleverness in recognizing it and said, out loud, "Alpini."

The officer looked surprised. Then he stopped talking and rose to his feet, and came round the table. She thought he was going to hit her, and flinched back into the arms of the soldiers. He peered intently at her face and said, in stiff English, "Your name, please."

She had forgotten a great deal, but she could manage that.

"I'm Laura," she said. "Laura Hart."

The Major said, "So?" Then he leaned forward and kissed her, first on one cheek, then on the other. It was an accolade. Then he started shouting, and men came running, and things became very confused. And then she was in a car, and then she was in a bedroom and a woman was helping her to strip off the filthy tattered remnants of her clothes and was giving her some tablets to swallow.

Hours, days, months later she was brought up out of the abyss of sleep by the sound of knocking. She lay there, with her eyes shut. There was something she had to do. Of course. She was going to stay with her brother, Charles, in Lienz, and she had asked the night porter to wake her, so that she could catch the Rome-Vienna express. What a party they had had the night before. How persistent Lorenz had been. How her head ached.

She opened her eyes, and the present came rushing back. She was in a neat little bedroom, paneled with pinewood. The knocker had opened the door and come in. It was a woman she remembered seeing vaguely the night before. And she had a pile of clothes in her arms. She said, in slow Italian, "We have hot water for you. The signora must hurry. The car comes in an hour."

In her bath, which was a long iron coffin in a sort of box room, Laura examined her body. Her feet and legs were cut, and her right ankle was still swollen. There were bruises on her stomach and breasts, which were beginning to turn black, and there was caked blood down the front of her body. The blood, as she discovered when she had washed it off, did not belong to her.

The clothes were an approximate fit. She had a feeling that they had belonged at one time to the Major's wife or, possibly, to one of his girl friends. She was finishing the coffee that had been brought

238

to her room when she heard a car draw up.

As she hurried down she suddenly remembered that she had no means of paying for anything. Her money, her passport, and a few personal possessions had been in a satchel, which might now be lying anywhere, in ten miles of mountain. It seemed odd to own nothing at all, not even the clothes she stood up in; odd, and curiously refreshing, like being born again.

The Major was waiting for her, and she tried to say something about money, but he waved it away and handed her into the car. He was driving himself, and he took her, fast, down miles of descending roads, into a town which she saw was called Tolmezzo.

There was a crowd at the railway station, and when she got out they started clapping and waving hands. She thought, at first, that the Major must be a very popular character, and then it seemed that she was the object of their attention.

She was still puzzling over this when the Major reappeared, forced a way through the crowd, which was growing thicker every moment, and handed her up into the train.

It was an empty, first-class carriage, and the guard was smiling at her, and locking the door on the corridor side. On the seat was a lunch basket and a pile of newspapers.

As if it had been waiting only for her, the train whistled and started. Laura lowered the window to wave to the kindly Major, and was surprised at the roar of welcome that greeted her. She continued to wave, since it seemed to be the thing to do, until the figures on the platform were a blur, whirled away as the train swung round a curve.

She took up the first paper, and found she was looking at her own face, enormously enlarged.

She recognized the photograph. It had been taken in the garden at home. She could see the French windows half open, and the handle of the garden roller. She wondered how an Italian newspaper could possibly have got hold of it, and then remembered that she had given a copy to Lorenz. There was another photograph below it. It showed the front of the theater and it showed too, clear enough even in the fuzzy reproduction, a gun sticking through the bottom of the turret window. As Laura read the story, it dawned on her that she was a heroine. Alone, and threatened by the powers of a police state, she had stood up for the truth, and vindicated it. More, by her courageous stand she had delayed the plans of a dictator; had delayed them fatally; had given the central power in Vienna time to restore control.

"The safety of the South Tyrol," said *Il Popolo*, "lay in her small hands, and she did not let it fall."

Laura looked at her small hands. They were cleaner than they had been, but they were still grubby, and the nails badly needed attention. Small hands. Black hands. Hands like the pad of a dog.

The newspaper slipped off her lap, and onto the floor.

When she woke up she realized she had been

asleep for a very long time indeed. Her mouth was dry, and her head was swimming with sleep. It felt like late afternoon, or early evening.

The guard reappeared with a carton of coffee. She gathered that she was now alone in the coach, which had been switched twice while she slept, once at Udine onto the Carinthia Express and again at Bologna onto the Rapide.

"Like the dead, you are asleep," said the guard. "Like the dead." Laura was astonished to see that there was a tear in the corner of each of his brown eyes.

She asked where they were, and gathered that they would be in Rome before long. "Una mezoretta," said the guard.

It was twenty minutes after this, and they were running through streets, when the train slowed and stopped. The door swung open, and Joe jumped in.

"Am I glad to see you!" he said, and kissed her warmly. She was happy to listen to him, and felt no desire to talk, until she remembered something, and said, "Did you kill them?"

Joe, who was describing a press reception planned for that evening, looked at her blankly.

"The photographer. The one whose shop was burnt down. And the frontier guard."

"Certainly not," said Joe. "The photographer was dead when I got there. And if his shop was burned down, it was done after I left. As for the frontier guard, he fell down and got his skis crossed. He may have broken an ankle. Why?"

But Laura found it difficult to say that she had seen so many violent deaths, four in the last two days, that even a single life spared, a single person alive who might have been dead, was a comforting item on the credit account. Being unable to explain this, she said nothing, and the train slid into the echoing cavern of Rome Central Station.

After that things got telescoped. There was a huge crowd. There were civic dignitaries. There was a colonel of carabinieri in a cocked hat. There were scores of newspapermen and hundreds of photographers. There were lights, and shouts, and a good deal of jostling, and over all the steady whirring of newsreel cameras. Then she was safe, in an enormous car, and a young man, in a neatly cut tweed suit who looked like a much younger version of Evelyn, was sitting on the seat beside her.

"We're going to the Embassy," he said. "Sir Harry wants to have a word with you before you make a statement."

"Have I got to make a statement?"

"I think it'll be expected of you. The thing Sir Harry wants to impress on you is that we don't want to offend the Austrian central government, or the Lienzers. They've settled all their differences now, and the last thing we want to do is to exacerbate them."

He looked absurdly young; younger even than Charles. And rather nice.

"If I'm going to give a press conference," she said, "I shall have to have some proper clothes. Do you think you could get me some?"

He said, "I think I could manage, if you could let me have your—er—particulars."

He looked so splendidly correct as he said this that Laura couldn't help laughing. And after a moment he laughed too. They were both laughing as the car turned in at the gates of the British Embassy.

There's an epidemic with 27 million victims. And no visible symptoms.

It's an epidemic of people who can't read.

Believe it or not, 27 million Americans are functionally illiterate, about one adult in five.

The solution to this problem is you... when you join the fight against illiteracy. So call the Coalition for Literacy at toll-free **1-800-228-8813** and volunteer.

**Volunteer
Against Illiteracy.
The only degree you need
is a degree of caring.**

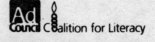